# He closed his eyes and let the memories come...

Memories of last night's lovemaking. For most of his life he'd focused on his career. Women came and went with the job and the location. No one had ever managed to keep a piece of his heart.

The idea rattled him hard, but it was the truth, the one ideal he'd always clung to. Truth, honor, courage. Those words meant a great deal to him. Honestly, three years ago Melissa hadn't needed a man like him, nor did she now.

Jonathan had sworn that he would never commit emotionally to anyone after that mission five years ago. He completed his assignments and went home—wherever home was. He made no attachments.

Then he'd met Melissa. Bit by tiny bit, she'd taken a part of him. She'd given of herself completely...and he hadn't been able to cut it.

He didn't deserve her forgiveness and he damn sure hadn't deserved her trust the way she'd given it last night. Hurting her again was the last thing he wanted to do. Maybe, just maybe, if he brought her niece back home safely, he'd earn all that Melissa had given him.

Finding Polly alive might just be impossible. But he had to try. For the child and for Melissa.

# DEBRA WEBB

## MISSING

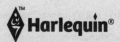

TORONTO NEW YORK LONDON
AMSTERDAM PARIS SYDNEY HAMBURG
STOCKHOLM ATHENS TOKYO MILAN MADRID
PRAGUE WARSAW BUDAPEST AUCKLAND

This story is dedicated to the real Melissa and Jonathan. As you take each other's hand in marriage, I wish you the most wonderful storybook ending of all!

ISBN-13: 978-0-373-69537-9

MISSING

Copyright © 2011 by Debra Webb

Recycling programs for this product may not exist in your area.

This edition published by arrangement with Harlequin Books S.A.

For questions and comments about the quality of this book please contact us at Customer_eCare@Harlequin.ca.

® and TM are trademarks of the publisher. Trademarks indicated with ® are registered in the United States Patent and Trademark Office, the Canadian Trade Marks Office and in other countries.

www.eHarlequin.com

**Printed in U.S.A.**

# ABOUT THE AUTHOR

Debra Webb wrote her first story at age nine and her first romance at thirteen. It wasn't until she spent three years working for the military behind the Iron Curtain and within the confining political walls of Berlin, Germany, that she realized her true calling. A five-year stint with NASA on the space shuttle program reinforced her love of the endless possibilities within her grasp as a storyteller. A collision course between suspense and romance was set. Debra has been writing romantic suspense and action-packed romantic thrillers since. Visit her at www.DebraWebb.com or write to her at P.O. Box 4889, Huntsville, AL 35815.

## Books by Debra Webb

HARLEQUIN INTRIGUE

934—THE HIDDEN HEIR*
951—A COLBY CHRISTMAS*
983—A SOLDIER'S OATH^
989—HOSTAGE SITUATION^
995—COLBY VS. COLBY^
1023—COLBY REBUILT*
1042—GUARDIAN ANGEL*
1071—IDENTITY UNKNOWN*
1092—MOTIVE: SECRET BABY
1108—SECRETS IN FOUR CORNERS
1145—SMALL-TOWN SECRETS ‡
1151—THE BRIDE'S SECRETS ‡
1157—HIS SECRET LIFE ‡
1173—FIRST NIGHT*
1188—COLBY LOCKDOWN**
1194—COLBY JUSTICE**
1216—COLBY CONTROL #
1222—COLBY VELOCITY #
1241—COLBY BRASS##
1247—COLBY CORE##
1270—MISSING+

* Colby Agency
^ The Equalizers
‡ Colby Agency: Elite Reconnaissance Division
** Colby Agency: Under Siege
# Colby Agency: Merger
##Colby Agency: Christmas Miracles
+Colby Agency: The New Equalizers

# CAST OF CHARACTERS

*Jonathan Foley*—As one of the new Equalizers, Jonathan must help Melissa find her missing niece—but can he do it without losing his wounded heart?

*Melissa Shepherd*—As a nurse, Melissa attends to the sick and injured every day of her life. But she can't seem to heal her own heart...the one Jonathan Foley shattered three years ago.

*Polly Shepherd*—This little girl is missing.

*William Shepherd*—His child is missing. But did he have anything to do with it?

*Harry Shepherd*—William and Melissa's uncle. He will do anything to keep William home from Afghanistan.

*Presley Shepherd*—She swears she was at home when her daughter was abducted in the middle of the night.

*Reed Talbot*—He's the chief of police. It's his job to find this missing child, not some hotshots from out of town.

*Carol Talbot*—She lost her only child. Can she survive watching her husband investigate this too-similar tragedy?

*Johnny Ray Bruce*—He is in competition with William for Presley. He intends to win...even if he has to do it with the nastiest kind of blackmail.

*Stevie Price*—He went missing the same day as the child. Is he a harmless mentally challenged man or something far more sinister?

*Floyd Harper*—He is the only witness to Stevie's alibi.

*Scott Rayburn*—He's the town's rich-boy lawyer. He knows everyone's secrets.

*Slade Keaton*—Slade isn't his real name, but he now owns the Equalizers. But his primary agenda isn't about the Equalizers at all...he has plans for the Colby Agency.

*Victoria Colby-Camp*—She has no idea that her world is about to be turned upside down.

*Lucas Camp*—He will do anything to protect his family.

# Chapter One

There were better ways to die.

But never a good time.

Jonathan Foley wouldn't have chosen to die in a vacant warehouse with the river lapping at its crumbling foundation. Definitely not while shackled to a cast-off swivel chair beneath the glare of a single bare bulb.

But life stunk that way sometimes.

"Amp it up another notch," the punk gripping the defibrillator paddles ordered. Then he smiled at his prisoner. "Last chance, tough guy."

Evidently the trigger-happy lackey was through playing. Foley braced for the electrical charge that would throttle through his chest the instant the paddles touched his naked skin. Nope, there was never a good time to die. But then he had accomplished his mission. This was likely as good a time as any. He lifted his gaze to the nimrod currently holding the power. "We both know I'm not going to talk."

The jerk laughed, his pale blue eyes glittering with anticipation. "I was hoping you'd say that."

The one manning the controls gave the appropriate knob a violent twist then checked the readout. "Ready," he announced.

Jonathan's jaw clenched and his fingers tightened on the arms of the chair, but he refused to close his eyes. He stared straight at the SOB with the paddles. Refused to allow even a glimmer of fear or defeat. This waste of DNA might kill him but he couldn't make him cooperate. Better men had tried.

"Stand down."

The sharply issued order echoed in the stale air of the long-abandoned warehouse, wiped the smile right off the paddle punk's face.

Foley should have relaxed. After all, he was just a few volts from dead. This unexpected interruption provided a momentary reprieve. He shifted his attention in the direction of the footsteps coming nearer. Not that he needed visual confirmation. He knew the voice.

Victor Lennox.

Tall, distinguished, with just enough gray at the temples to lend an air of wisdom. Even at a time like this—in a place like this—the man sported a three thousand dollar black silk suit. No doubt the leather shoes he wore were handcrafted. Nothing was too good for a Lennox. A similarly dressed underling, briefcase in hand, rushed after him.

Well, well, Foley mused. Would wonders never cease? He'd thought Lennox was long gone by now. Yet, here he was, in the flesh, assistant in tow.

"Sir," the underling urged, "the Learjet is waiting. There's no time."

Lennox held up a hand, cutting off his much younger colleague. "Before you die," Lennox said to Foley, his gaze narrowed with disdain and fury, "I have one question."

Foley licked his cracked lips, noted the taste of blood and sweat. "For the past two hours I've been beaten—" his ribs ached with each indrawn breath "—shocked with ever increasing amperage and—" he jerked his head toward the punk with the paddles "—I still didn't talk. What makes you think I have anything to say to you?"

"Let me give it another go," paddle punk pleaded. "He'll talk." He smirked at Foley. "They always do."

Lennox shook his head firmly from side to side. "Not this one."

"Sir." The assistant dared to intrude into the exchange yet again. "You must hurry."

Lennox ignored him. "I did my research, Foley. I know all about you." He made a disparaging sound deep in his throat. "And you're right, you won't talk." He crossed his arms over his chest then reached up and tapped his chin with a finger as if mulling over the situation. "I have friends in places you can't even fathom. I'm aware of your military career, *Major* Foley."

One corner of Foley's mouth twitched with the ghost of a smile. "Then you know it was over a long time ago." Bits and pieces of images flickered through his brain. He banished the memories.

"You endured days of torture," Lennox went on as if recalling documents he'd only just recently read. "Never uttered a single word while every member of your reconnaissance team was executed right in front of you." A hint of respect flashed in the man's eyes. "Still you remained strong. Loyal to the bitter end. Didn't let your country down." He gave another shake of that distinguished head. "No, no. You didn't talk then. You won't talk now."

"Then what's your point?" Foley looked him dead in the eye. He would have a point. A man who'd just been nailed for treason wasn't going to hang around for anything without a compelling reason.

"After a few years of doing nothing significant, you joined a firm called the Equalizers," Lennox explained, as if he had all night and wasn't the slightest bit worried about the feds who no doubt had already turned Chicago upside down to find him. "Your most recent assignment was to do what no one else had been able to do."

"That's right." Foley had gotten Lennox. Gotten him good. No one else had been able to penetrate the perfect shield he'd built around himself. No one had

had a clue that it was the esteemed Victor Lennox who was selling out his own company, his own country. Now his crimes were bared to all. He could run, but he would never again possess the power he had flaunted. Checkmate.

Lennox leaned down, stuck his face in Foley's. "Who sent you?"

"The head of the Equalizers."

Rage tightened the features of the man's face better than the Botox he likely used on a regular basis. "Three people were involved in that aspect of my business," Lennox hissed. "Only three. Not one of them sold me out."

Foley shrugged. "I guess you'll never know for sure."

"Oh, I already know. You see, every man has his breaking point. Each of the three broke eventually. Like you, they remained loyal until the end. Though I suspect they were motivated by fear rather than anything else. You," he accused, "already knew coming in what you were after. All you had to do was find concrete evidence."

Foley stared at him. He wasn't denying or confirming that assertion.

"It's not necessary for you to corroborate the statement," Lennox assured him. "I know."

"Mr. Lennox," the well-dressed assistant interrupted again, "we must go. *Now.*"

Continuing to discount the warning, Lennox demanded, "Tell me who sent you."

That ghost of a smile materialized fully on Foley's lips. "I told you. My employer—the head of the Equalizers."

"A name, Foley," Lennox pressed. "I want a name."

Foley could tell him that he didn't know, because he didn't. No one did. The man behind the Equalizers was a complete unknown. So Foley did what he did best. He said nothing.

"You've won," Lennox fairly shouted. "I've been exposed. I'm on the run. Even I know that it's only a matter of time before they catch up with me. What difference does it make now? I simply want to know the identity of the man who discovered what no one else could."

Foley wondered if Lennox had any idea just how much satisfaction his sheer desperation prompted.

"Cut him loose," Lennox ordered.

"What?" the paddle punk demanded.

"Sir!" the assistant declared, his panic clearly mounting.

"He's going with us," Lennox announced. "I will know who sent him." He stared directly at Foley once more. "Every man has his breaking point. All I need is time to find yours."

While the assistant argued with Lennox, the punk tossed aside the paddles and reached for the knife lying on the cart next to the controls. He grumbled curses under his breath but followed the order. His cohort passed a handgun to Lennox.

Lennox waved the weapon toward the rear door through which he'd entered. "Let's go."

Foley pushed to his feet, the pain radiating through his muscles and settling deep into his bones.

Lennox nudged him in the side with the weapon. "Move," he commanded.

Foley had taken two steps when a cell phone blasted a familiar tune. He glanced over his shoulder at the phone lying on the table next to the portable defibrillator. *His* phone. He'd been relieved of his weapon, his wallet and his phone hours ago.

"Check the screen," Lennox directed.

Foley resisted the urge to roll his eyes. Wouldn't matter if it was his employer, the name and number would reveal nothing. A trace on the call would divulge the same.

"No name," paddle punk reported as he scrutinized the screen. "Out of area call."

A frown attempted to stretch across Foley's brow but he schooled the expression. His employer's number usually showed up as a local call. A different number every time.

"Accept the call," Lennox instructed his torture technician, "and put it on speaker." He glanced around the room. "Not a word from anyone."

The creep holding Foley's cell punched the necessary buttons.

Another waste of time. Foley's employer wouldn't leave a voice mail or speak into dead air. Maybe if Lennox wasted enough time, the feds would be waiting for him at whatever airfield where his Learjet waited on standby.

"Hello, Jonathan…"

Emotion exploded in Foley's chest. Three years… three long years of sleepless nights and pent-up frustration leached into his blood. Haunting snippets of whispered words, the brushing of lips and the hot, smooth feel of bare skin against bare skin rushed into his brain.

It couldn't be…

"I hope this is your voice mail…" A shaky release of breath sighed across the silence. "Call me, please." She stumbled through a number. "I…I need your help. *Please.* It's a matter of life and death."

Silence reigned for three beats, then Lennox smiled. "Ah. Perhaps we've found the missing piece we need." Certainty glinted in his eyes.

Foley's mind churned with emotions. Why would she call him now?

Didn't matter. He knew her inside and out.

Something was very wrong.

Lennox nudged Foley in the spleen with the weapon. "That sounded exactly like the sort of leverage I need to obtain the answer to my question."

Ice formed in Foley's gut. No way was he letting this ruthless monster learn her identity and use her.

"Bring me that cell phone," Lennox ordered his underling. He reached out in anticipation of having it placed in his palm.

Foley whipped around and in one second had

Lennox in a chokehold, the weapon he still gripped aimed at his proud brow. "Don't ever let yourself be distracted when you've got a gun to a man's back."

Paddle punk's cohort dared to reach for his weapon.

"Nobody moves," Foley warned. He bored the barrel of the nine millimeter into Lennox's temple.

Both men inched forward, testing the line Foley had drawn.

"Do as he says!" Lennox squeaked around the pressure on his throat.

Smart man. "You," Foley said to the underling who'd followed Lennox into the warehouse, "call 911 and give our location. Then give me my cell."

Weapons clattered to the floor as the two thugs who'd tortured Foley raised their hands in surrender. "You got what you want," the one who'd brandished the paddles said. "You don't need us." The two started backing away, most likely toward an exit somewhere beyond the scope of the single bare bulb's illumination.

"You're right." Foley studied the two men. "But you're walking away from your best chance at cutting a deal," he warned. "Your prints are all over the place." He nodded to the tools of the torture trade. "Chances are the police will find you eventually."

Paddle punk's eyes narrowed. "What kind of deal?"

Now that was loyalty. "I'm sure the DA will be very interested in any details the two of you can give regarding his—" he tightened his hold on Lennox "—activities. Your cooperation could earn you a very sweet deal."

Lennox attempted to blubber his own warning. Foley clamped his arm tighter around the bastard's throat and shot a look at the man who'd trailed in here after him like a puppy. "Make the call," Foley repeated.

While the assistant in the expensive suit entered the necessary digits, the two thugs dropped to their knees then went face down on the concrete floor.

"You might think you've won," Lennox screeched, "but you and your employer will suffer the consequences."

"Maybe." Foley nodded to the guy who'd made the 911 call. "Bring my cell to me," he ordered a second time, "then join your pals on the floor."

The younger man glanced at the filthy floor then swallowed hard.

"Now," Foley prompted.

The man inched close enough to give Foley the phone, then side-stepped in those same small increments back toward his partners in crime. It was almost worth the torture Foley had endured to watch that silk suit kiss the dirt and, during the short minutes before the cops arrived, to listen to Lennox's offers of excessive amounts of cash for his freedom.

But Foley had one thing on his mind. *Her.* She'd called. Unbelievable. He hadn't seen her, hadn't heard her voice in three years.

*I need your help.*

Worry throbbed in his skull, flexed in his jaw.

She wouldn't call him…unless it truly was a matter of life and death.

Fear trickled into his veins.

He had to get to her.

When the cops arrived, Foley gave one of the officers his business card and walked away. He ignored the warning that he wasn't supposed to leave until the detective in charge of the case arrived.

There wasn't a force on earth that could prevent him from going.

The cell in his pocket sang its annoying tune.

Foley withdrew it, checked the display in case it was her calling again.

It wasn't. It was his employer.

Not at all surprised his employer already knew Lennox was down—he seemed hotwired into everywhere with everyone—Foley hit the answer button even as he quickened his pace. "Foley."

"Outstanding job," the voice on the other end praised. "I knew you were the right man for this one. File your final report and relax. I'll contact the office with your next assignment."

What kind of man could position a player to bring down a man like Lennox? A god in the murky and political world of government contractors.

"Who are you?" Foley had been hired as an Equalizer more than five months ago. He'd heard this voice a dozen times, but he had no idea who the guy was or even what he looked like. Foley and the other two Equalizers currently on staff had done their research, gone to all sorts of lengths to find that answer.

And there was nothing. It was as if the man behind the voice didn't exist.

"One day you'll know," the voice promised. "For now, your payment will be deposited into your bank account today."

The connection severed.

Foley stalled, stared at the phone a moment. One day he would know? What did that mean? Then he shook off the questions and broke into a sprint.

*She* needed him.

He shouldn't care.

Stepping back into her life would be a mistake... for both of them.

But he couldn't ignore the call.

Not even if he tried.

# Chapter Two

Calling *him* had been a last resort.

Melissa Shepherd hugged her arms around her middle and stared through the window over the kitchen sink at the drizzling rain. She was desperate.

Or crazy.

She shuddered. Jonathan Foley had disappeared from her life three years ago. The ache, though dull, still swelled deep inside her whenever he came to mind. She shouldn't have called him. Bay Minette's entire police force, aided by numerous volunteers from surrounding towns and counties, hadn't been able to find her niece, so why in the world would she believe he could?

Misery washed over Melissa. Polly had been missing for five days. Five endless days and nights.

Melissa's brother was scheduled to ship back to Afghanistan on Tuesday, the day after Memorial Day. She shook her head. How could he leave with his three-year-old daughter missing? The military didn't seem to care.

Closing her eyes, Melissa blew out a heavy breath. That wasn't fair. It wasn't that they didn't care. Her brother, William, was trained in a highly critical MOS—military occupational skill. It was a miracle he'd even gotten this too-short, two-week leave in the first place.

That was the real reason Melissa had called Jonathan. He didn't like talking about his past career in the military but, from what she'd gathered, during that time he had been connected to extremely high-level people—important people. He could call someone. She was certain of it.

She'd asked him to do that when he'd returned her call in the middle of the night last night. He'd promised to call her back this morning.

So far she hadn't heard a word.

Melissa opened her eyes and searched the back-yard of her childhood home, her heart automatically hoping her gaze would land on sweet little Polly playing there. But the yard was empty. The old rope and wood swing her father had built for her as a child hung empty from the big old pecan tree's massive branch.

She'd tried. For days Melissa and the rest of the family, along with friends and neighbors, had searched. And nothing. It was as if Polly had vanished into thin air, leaving no trace of the reason for, or the person behind, her disappearance.

Other than the fact that Stevie was missing, too.
Melissa shook her head. She couldn't believe that
Stevie would ever harm Polly. He loved her. Stevie
Price had suffered immense cruelty and severe
trauma as an infant. The physical trauma had resulted
in brain damage, leaving him mentally challenged.
By the time he was four his self-centered mother had
abandoned him. His father had tried to take care of
him, but he'd had problems of his own. When Stevie
was nineteen his father had died. He'd lived off the
kindness of folks in the community ever since. And
though he was thirty now, his mind was like a child's.
The children in the community loved Stevie.

Melissa had played with him as a kid.

He wouldn't do this.

Someone else was responsible for this horror.

Hadn't the Shepherd family suffered enough
tragedy? First her father had been killed by serving
his country while she and William were just kids.
Melissa was convinced that was the reason William
insisted on joining the military in the first place—
to somehow feel closer to his father. Then, as if that
hadn't been a kick in the teeth, their mother had
died four years ago. Melissa hadn't been anywhere
near ready to lose her mother. But Polly had come
along and she'd brought new light to that dark, empty
place.

Now she was missing. After five days Melissa
feared the worst.

A lump rose, tightening her throat. *Please, God, don't let that sweet baby be hurt.*

As if her agony had summoned him, William came up beside her. "The chief sent me home."

Melissa turned to her brother. He looked beyond exhausted. She knew full well the agony she felt was nothing compared to what he suffered. Polly was his first and only child. He loved her more than life itself. He'd done everything in his power to give her a good life—in spite of the difficulties he and his wife had in their marriage.

The whole town despised Presley. Whispered ugly things behind William's back when he'd announced that he and Presley were to be married. Melissa wasn't blind or stupid. She knew full well the stories, some all too true, that traveled the gossip circuit on a regular basis about her sister-in-law. But Melissa chose to give Presley the benefit of the doubt. Everyone deserved a second chance and Presley'd had a rough go of it as a kid. William loved her. That was enough for Melissa.

"Presley was sleeping," William said, his voice weak with fatigue and fierce worry. "I didn't want to bother her so I came here."

Melissa's chest tightened. Whatever anyone thought of Presley, she worshipped Polly. As much of a nightmare as this was for her, Melissa couldn't begin to fathom how Presley felt. "You need sleep, too." She brushed the back of her hand across his shadowed jaw. He felt cold despite the unseasonably warm weather. "You can't help Polly if you're too worn out to think straight."

William shook his head. "I can't bear to sleep." Emotion glistened in his bloodshot eyes. "Who would do this?" His lips trembled. "Who would take my baby?" He dropped his head.

The sheer agony in his voice tore at Melissa's heart. Just looking at him brought images of Polly to mind. The little girl had her daddy's blond hair and blue eyes. She was a little duplicate of him and she'd brought so much joy to their lives.

The loud chime of the doorbell echoed through the too-quiet house.

Melissa's and William's gazes locked.

What if they'd found Polly or…Melissa swallowed tightly…her body?

*Dear God, no, no, no. Don't let that be.*

Melissa pulled her bravado up off the floor and wrapped it around her. "They would've called," she said aloud. That was right. She let the air seep back into her lungs. "If they'd found her, they would've called." The courage she'd dredged up and the words she'd spoken for her brother's benefit did nothing to slow the thundering in her chest.

William nodded. "Guess so."

The chime echoed a second time. "Stay here." Melissa squeezed his arm. "I'll see who it is."

She turned from her brother, her heart somehow rising into her throat while it continued to pound frantically, and started toward the living room. The dishes she'd intended to wash when she'd come into the kitchen still waited, but she didn't care. It was difficult to keep her mind on anything except Polly.

Chief Talbot, the town's chief of police since Melissa was a kid, had ordered Melissa back home this morning, too. He didn't want her or William out there. Maybe because of what he feared finding or maybe just because they both looked like death warmed over.

At least the chief had allowed their Uncle Harry to continue helping with the search. Harry would call the instant he knew anything. He was practically a second father to her and William. He'd stepped in when their father was killed, taking over for the younger brother he'd adored. Melissa felt certain that was why he'd never married and had a family of his own. He'd been too busy taking care of his younger brother's.

Holding her breath, Melissa opened the front door.

She'd braced for the appearance of one of Bay Minette's finest or a family friend bearing bad news.

But not this. She wasn't prepared for this.

Jonathan Foley.

The breath she'd been holding whispered past her lips, his name forming there without conscious thought. "Jonathan."

"Melissa."

The sound of his voice echoed through her being,

made her soul ache with the need to reach out to him. He looked exactly the same. Tall with shoulders that filled the doorway. Thick black hair still military short. Chiseled jaw that gave the impression of unyielding stone. But it was the eyes that made her already pounding heart stumble drunkenly.

They were ice blue, so pale they were almost gray. She'd always been certain that he could see right through her. That he could read her every thought.

"I've been waiting for you to call." She managed to keep her voice steady, which was an outright miracle.

"May I come in?"

Shaking off the shock and confusion, Melissa stepped back. "Of course." *Get your head together, girl.*

Jonathan Foley stepped across the threshold and into her family home. Melissa's breath deserted her once more. He was here. After nearly three years without a word, he was here.

He waited patiently, his eyes searching hers.

She summoned the courage that had apparently run for parts unknown. "I'm glad you came." It was the truth. She'd expected nothing more than a phone call but she was damned glad he was here. The urge to fall into his arms consumed her again.

"Has there been any word on your niece?"

Melissa moved her head side to side. The movement felt stiff and jerky with the tension ruthlessly gripping her neck.

Silence pressed against her, filled the room for half a dozen beats of her aching heart.

She gave herself a mental kick. "Please sit." She gestured to the sofa and chairs. Wherever he lived now, whatever his job or personal status, he'd come to Alabama to help her family. For that she felt immensely grateful.

He waited for her to take a seat first, then he settled in the chair directly across from her position on the sofa. Old, well-worn, the sofa had been around since she was a kid. The upholstery had changed a couple of times, ending up a wild mix of pink and red flowers against a green and white background. Her mother had picked it out and Melissa didn't have the heart to change it.

Jonathan considered her a moment, his posture straight and rigid as if he expected a general to enter the room at any moment and he might have to jump to his feet and salute. His forearms rested along the length of the chair arms, his hands palms down, his long fingers extended as if that were the only part of him fully relaxed. Then he finally spoke. "She's been missing for five days?"

"Yes." That sinking feeling that bottomed out in her stomach each time Melissa thought about sweet little Polly out there alone or worse dropped like a stone deep into her belly now. "They're continuing to search for her." She shook her head. "But they haven't found anything yet."

His gaze narrowed so very slightly that she might

have missed the change if she hadn't been staring so intently at him. "No suspects? No evidence discovered?"

"Nothing at all." She clenched her fingers together and pressed her fists into her lap to prevent them from shaking.

"Has the FBI been called in to assist?"

Melissa had to really concentrate to pull the answer from the mass of painful and confusing information she'd attempted to process the past few days. "There was talk of someone coming from Montgomery." What had the chief said? Her mind was a total blank! What was wrong with her? Taking a deep breath, she finally pieced it together. "I think a consult was done by phone."

She waited for a response, physical or verbal, but he said nothing. Sat utterly still. Analyzing her answer, she supposed.

Memories flooded her brain. Moments shared with this man that she had shared with no other human being. Secrets…feelings. *Stop.* She ordered herself back to the matter of importance. "Is that normal procedure?" she asked when he continued to sit stone still without saying a word.

"Sometimes." He paused a moment as if to be sure of his words. "The Bureau's involvement is strictly on a case by case basis. If they're not on the scene they feel there is nothing their presence could add at this point."

Did that mean the FBI felt Polly's case was

hopeless? Before Melissa could ask as much, he said, "Walk me through exactly what happened."

Where was William? Melissa glanced at the door that separated the kitchen and dining room from the living room. Forcing him to relive that night would only add to his misery. "It was late. William and his wife had a fight." Melissa took a moment to tamp down the renewed rush of emotion. "You know how young couples can be. A little too much passion and not quite enough common sense. William didn't want Polly to be awakened by the arguing so he left and came here for the night." Melissa's throat attempted to close again. "The next morning when he went home Polly was gone and Presley was sleeping off the vodka she'd used to drown her frustrations."

More than one well-meaning neighbor had commented that no decent mother would drink herself unconscious with her child in the next room. But that was the main emotional outlet Presley had been exposed to growing up. It was what she knew. Melissa wanted to shake her every time she thought about it, but that wouldn't change a thing.

Even more troubling, the house had been unlocked when William arrived home that awful morning. William insisted he had locked up when he left. Presley claimed he clearly had not since the back door had been wide open with no indication of forced entry. Melissa wanted to believe William, but he'd been damned upset that night. He was only human.

Sweet Jesus, how could this have happened?

"He called the police," Jonathan prompted.

"Yes." Melissa chewed at her bottom lip. Her throat was so dry she could scarcely breathe much less swallow. "The chief and one of his deputies arrived within minutes. William and Presley were arguing." Melissa shook her head. "It was terrible...just terrible."

Another long moment of tension-filled silence passed, with Jonathan watching her, assessing her. What was he thinking? Had he already formed some sort of conclusion? How was that possible? He didn't know her family. Certainly she'd mentioned her brother and niece, and her uncle, but Jonathan hadn't bothered to stick around long enough to meet any of them. Melissa had been living and working in Birmingham at the time. Still would be if her mother hadn't gotten sick and then if her brother hadn't deployed to the Middle East.

William had begged Melissa to come home and keep an eye on Polly. And Presley. Determined to help, Melissa had come home and still this unthinkable tragedy had occurred.

"The investigation has uncovered nothing?" her visitor asked again.

"Nothing." It was disheartening, awful even, but it was the truth. "No one saw anything or heard anything," she explained, hoping to make herself perfectly clear this time. "Whoever took Polly left no evidence. Nothing."

"I spoke to my contact at the Pentagon."

A little hitch disrupted her respiration. "And?" This was what she'd called him about, what she'd needed from him. Not this interrogation. His questions felt exactly like that. As if he was interrogating her. Stay calm, she ordered herself. He was trying to help. Her fingernails pinched into her palms.

"Your brother's orders have been put on hold indefinitely."

Relief flooded Melissa with such force her shoulders trembled. "Thank you."

"But…"

Fear and something resembling anger swirled fast and furiously in Melissa's stomach. "But?" This was going to be something she wouldn't like. She could feel it. Jonathan's hesitation spoke volumes.

"If your brother was somehow involved," Jonathan warned, "there will be serious consequences."

Melissa blinked. At first his words just sort of bounced off the wad of emotions swaddling her brain. Then the realization filtered through. He was suggesting William was somehow involved with Polly's disappearance. "What?" She couldn't have heard him right. There had to be a mistake. The very idea was ludicrous.

Jonathan didn't look away. His gaze held hers with the same ferocity as when she'd first found him standing outside the door. "It happens, Melissa."

The way he said her name, with that same thick huskiness as when they'd made love, ripped open the wounds she'd thought long healed and forgotten.

"More often than you know," he went on while she scrambled to regain her equilibrium. "These soldiers experience things…see things that change them from the inside out. Sometimes they can't accept the idea of going back. They'll do anything to ensure that doesn't happen. The suicide rate is incredibly high."

She couldn't move, couldn't respond. Melissa knew her brother. No matter what he'd experienced, he would never, ever put his daughter in harm's way. Never. Anyone who suggested such a thing either didn't know him or was a fool.

"Most of the families feel that way, even after the worst has happened."

His answer told her she'd stated her thoughts aloud. Looking down, she unclenched her fingers and swiped her palms against her jean-clad thighs before clenching her fingers into fists once more. Meeting his gaze would take some regrouping. He couldn't be right. No way. William would never do that. He'd been questioned along those very lines the same day he'd discovered Polly was missing. He wouldn't, couldn't do it.

"You're wrong." Her gaze locked with Jonathan's once more. "William would sacrifice himself in a heartbeat for his child. No way would he do this."

"War changes people. Some more than others, but no one is exempt. Whether it's visible or not, the change is there." Jonathan took a deep breath, the rise and fall of his chest the first indication that he had even that essential human need. "The only person who can be certain of William now is William himself."

Melissa opened her mouth to defend her brother but never got the chance.

"He's right."

She twisted around to look at William. The idea that he might have overheard all that had been said in the last few minutes wrenched her heart.

"Sergeant Shepherd," Jonathan acknowledged.

"Major Foley." William stepped past Melissa and settled into the chair next to hers.

"It's just Foley now," Jonathan corrected.

William made a sound in his throat, not quite a laugh. "Are you sure?"

Melissa watched the interaction between the two men, her pulse thumping in her ears. The connection between the two was instantaneous and palpable. They'd never met, yet the military connection somehow made them familiar.

One corner of Jonathan's mouth quirked with an almost smile. "You've got me there. But today we're not soldiers so let's keep things informal."

William gave an agreeable nod. "My daughter is my heart," he said, his tone flat. His emotions had run so high for the past few days that his mind and body could no longer maintain the necessary energy for emotional nuances. "I would gladly die right now if it would bring her back here."

"I have no doubt," Jonathan concurred. "However,

even the best of us have moments when we snap. Maybe do something we didn't intend to do." Before William could counter, he added, "Then denial kicks in and we genuinely don't believe ourselves capable of such an act. The mind is a powerful thing. It sometimes protects us from that which we cannot bear."

Unlike Jonathan, William's shoulders were slumped, his usually handsome face lined with fatigue. He turned his hands, palms up. "Believe what you choose, Foley. I had nothing to do with my baby's disappearance." His voice cracked with the last. "My only guilt is in not being there like I should have been."

Melissa took his hand in hers. His felt limp and cold. "You don't have to convince anyone," she soothed. "He just doesn't know you, that's all." She glared at the man she'd called to help. "Thank you for making that call." She squared her shoulders. "Right now William and I should get down to the command post and see what we can do to help." Melissa didn't care what the chief said, she wasn't going to sit here and do nothing.

She absolutely was not going to put William through another interrogation.

Jonathan stood. "I'm glad I could help."

Every fiber of her being screamed at her to say something, to stop him from leaving. But she wanted him to go, didn't she? He'd made the call. William didn't have to leave until Polly was found. Melissa didn't need anything else from Jonathan. He should go.

William pushed to his feet, letting go of Melissa's hand and reaching for Jonathan's. "Sir, you don't know how much I appreciate what you've done." He shook Jonathan's hand with a firmness that Melissa would have thought him too weary to generate at this point. "I have no qualms about serving my country." His hand fell back to his side. "I just couldn't go… yet."

Jonathan nodded. "When this is resolved, let me know and I'll make the necessary calls."

"Yes, sir."

Jonathan strode toward the door.

Melissa's feet remained glued to the floor all the way up until the moment he opened the door.

She was across the room and calling after him before her brain caught up with her actions. "Jonathan." What the hell was she doing? She should let him go!

He stopped, nearly to the steps, and turned, that ice blue gaze colliding with hers.

"We're scared." She pressed her lips together a moment and fought to hold back the tears. "We… we've never been in a situation like this. We don't know if the police are doing everything they can do." She shrugged, tried to hold back some of the truth spilling out of her, but that wasn't happening. "We ask questions and get answers we don't understand. We try to help but they…"

Jonathan was coming back toward her, one steady

step at a time, his gaze never leaving hers, not even to blink.

"They don't know anything…" A sob halted her words. "They can't tell us anything except to be patient and to pray." Frankly, she was beginning to doubt her link to the Almighty. She'd about prayed herself out, about lost hope.

Jonathan stopped toe-to-toe with her. "It's possible that what the police are telling you is all there is to tell." He shook his head slowly, somberly. "These cases can go unsolved for years." A shadow moved across his face. "I have to tell you, after five days, if there's been no ransom demand, the chances of the child being found alive are slim to none."

"Polly." The name trembled on Melissa's lips.

A frown line formed between his eyebrows.

"That's her name," Melissa said. "She's three years old and the most precious child." She smiled even as a hot tear slid down her cheek. "She has to be alive. I'm not willing to accept anything else. If—" Another of those halting sobs caught her words. "If you can help us, it would mean a great deal to me if you would stay."

The morning breeze whispered across her skin, sending goose bumps scattering up her arms. She waited for his answer, prayed some more in spite of herself. Maybe he couldn't help, but somehow, deep in her heart, she knew that his presence would make a difference. She had denied that knowledge, had told herself she'd called him just for the military connection, but that had been a lie.

She needed him right now. Melissa didn't want to admit any such thing, but it was true.

Damn it, it was true.

"Make no mistake," he said quietly, "I can't promise you anything."

She shook her head adamantly. "You don't have to promise anything. It's enough that you try." Her lungs dragged in a deep, much needed breath.

Their gazes held for one, two, three beats. "All right then. I'll try."

# Chapter Three

*11:05 a.m.*

Jonathan stayed on the front porch of William Shepherd's modest home while he and Melissa argued with his apparently uncooperative wife. The windows were raised, allowing the breeze to drift inside and also permitting the raised voices to carry right out to where Jonathan waited on the ancient wooden swing.

Presley's argument was simple. She'd been interviewed by the police twice, the family half a dozen times and she had no desire to answer questions from some friend of Melissa's. The way she said her sister-in-law's name suggested a serious dislike. In sharp contrast, Melissa patiently and gently urged Presley to reconsider.

*Melissa.*

Jonathan drew in a breath, the heaviness in his chest fighting the effort. What the hell was he doing here? He'd made the call. That was all she'd asked him to do when they'd spoken on the phone. Her brother now had whatever time he needed to resolve this terrible state of affairs. The local police seemed competent; the FBI had been consulted. There was little else Jonathan could do other than retrace already taken steps. He nudged the porch floorboards with the toe of his boot, setting the swing in motion.

And yet he had agreed to stay when she'd asked. Because he had to.

Jonathan closed his eyes and let the memories he'd dammed years ago flood his mind. Their meeting had been nothing more than a chance encounter. He'd been on the final plummet of a serious downhill slide. Walking away from his military career under the circumstances at the time of his official exodus had plunged him into a thirty-month descent of self-pity and denial. Denial of who he was and what he'd done.

Until a midnight brawl in a bar in Birmingham had landed him under arrest and with a nasty gash as a souvenir. He rubbed at his forehead where the scar still ached whenever he thought of his former stupidity.

Registered Nurse Melissa Shepherd had been on duty at the ER that night. She'd patched him up and, after he'd made bail, she'd said yes to his offer of dinner as a way of showing his gratitude for her extraordinary patience with a less than amiable patient.

The ability to draw in a deep breath deserted him once more as the memories poured through him. No one had ever pulled him in so deeply. He hadn't been able to get enough of touching her, of looking at her. He would have done anything for her—except put the past behind him and make a real commitment. The dreams—no, the nightmares—he'd suffered since that last military mission had prevented any possibility of moving on with his life. Jonathan Foley existed in the moment.

Even Melissa's unconditional love hadn't been enough at the time to help him move beyond the past. The facts listed in his official military jacket that explained the decisions—decisions he had made that protected the mission but ultimately cost the lives of good men. The same facts that still allowed him to call up a top-ranking official at the Pentagon and make things happen.

Jonathan surveyed the small yard that flanked the little house Melissa's brother called home. The picket fence needed a fresh coat of paint. The house could use one, too, but it was a home. Maybe not such a happy home, but a home where a man and woman had made a commitment to give life together a shot. A home where a child played. The colorful sandbox beneath the oak tree, along with the big plastic, equally colorful building blocks made for climbing marked this as a home where a child lived.

Except that child was missing. Probably deceased.

Regret twisted in Jonathan's gut.

Melissa didn't want to consider that possibility but

the chances the child was deceased were far greater than the likelihood that she would be found alive.

Melissa and her family didn't deserve this horrific pain. Unfortunately Jonathan doubted he would be able to make it right. He would try. He owed Melissa that. She had given everything she'd had to give and he'd walked away.

He'd let her down just as he had his team two years prior to that.

His work as an Equalizer now allowed him to do what he couldn't do over five years ago for his team, what he couldn't do for Melissa three years back. Make a wrong right.

Maybe if he could in some way make this tragic wrong right, he could forgive himself for hurting Melissa with such nonchalance.

He had to try.

The screen door opened and Melissa leaned out. "You can come in now."

Jonathan pressed the soles of his boots against the porch floor, stopping the swing and simultaneously pushing himself up.

"Just one thing." Melissa looked embarrassed. "Presley has a serious hangover. She's a little cranky so tread lightly."

"Yeah." Jonathan forced something as close to a smile as he could produce. "I got that part."

He immediately regretted the words. Melissa's look of weary exasperation had him rethinking his lack of tact. When she turned and went inside, he followed.

The interior of the house was as humble as the exterior, and equally in need of attention. Toys lay scattered about, but the glaring theme was disorderliness. Under the circumstances it was expected, but Jonathan sensed the house had always been untidy. Clearly, living up to "Suzy Homemaker" standards was not on Presley's agenda.

Presley Shepherd, twenty-three according to her DMV record, currently had auburn hair. Her DMV photo showed her as a blonde with a brazen blue streak down one side. She was dangerously thin and quite happy to show off as much of her slight frame as possible. The shorts and tank top were two sizes too small even for her.

"Presley," Melissa said, "this is my friend Jonathan."

The missing child's mother peered up from her perch on the sofa, her gaunt cheeks making her eyes appear inordinately large. "Let's just get this over with. I have stuff to do."

William indicated the end of the sectional sofa farthest away from where his wife lounged. "Please, have a seat, sir."

Jonathan waited for Melissa to settle first, then lowered onto the upholstered sofa beside her. The brush of his arm against hers made him flinch. Thankfully she didn't seem to notice.

"What do you wanna know?" Presley demanded.

She combed her fingers through her hair and looked him up and down as if she'd only just realized he was male.

"Why don't you walk me through the night Polly went missing," Jonathan suggested.

Presley rolled her eyes.

"I know this is hard," Melissa said softly, "but we have to try every avenue."

Jonathan was amazed by her patience. He wasn't so sure Presley deserved so much slack. He didn't need a shrink to analyze this woman. Her indifference and self-absorption were glaringly evident and, based on what he'd read of her background when he'd looked into the characters related to this drama, likely related to her neglected childhood.

"William and I had a big fight." Presley glanced at her husband, who looked as miserable as he no doubt felt. "Polly was asleep. I didn't want her waking up with us fighting again so he went to his folks' house for the night. No big mystery." She threw her hands up. "Same old, same old." She made eye contact with Jonathan only once and only briefly as she spoke.

"Again?" he asked.

Her pale face scrunched into a frown. "What?"

"You said," Jonathan clarified, "that you didn't want Polly to wake up with you fighting 'again.' Have you been fighting frequently?" He glanced from Presley to William and back. "Since he returned home on leave?"

Her thin, pointy shoulders hunched. "I don't know.

Yeah, I guess. We always fight." She looked to her husband. "It's just the way we are."

William said nothing.

Jonathan moved in a different direction. "According to the police report, there was no sign of forced entry. Did you ensure the door was locked after he left?"

She twirled the fingers of her right hand in her hair. "Course. I'd be stupid not to."

William cut a look at her but quickly glanced away.

Jonathan let several seconds lapse before broaching the next question. He wanted both of them to squirm a moment. William's posture and outward expression never changed. Presley's, on the other hand, became more agitated. She changed positions on the sofa twice and tugged at her skimpy blouse.

"Besides yourself and William who has a key to your house?"

William looked to Melissa. "You have one."

Melissa nodded. "I keep it in the key box at home." To Jonathan she added, "It's on the wall by the back door. That's where we hang the keys."

"No one else." William turned to Presley. "Right?"

"You'd know better than me," she said, incensed. "You got the locks changed the last time you were home."

Jonathan considered her statement a moment as she and her husband discussed the issue of keys.

"Why did you have the locks changed?" he asked, the question directed to William.

"Presley was being harassed by this jerk," William said, "and I was about to be deployed for six months." He shrugged. "I was trying to protect my family."

"Worked out real good, didn't it?" Presley snapped.

A new layer of agony settled deep into William's features.

"Blaming William or yourself won't help right now," Melissa said in that same gentle tone. "Is there any possibility someone else had a key? One of your friends maybe?"

Presley shot up from the sofa. "I knew this was the way it would be." She planted her hands on her narrow hips. "I've been through this crap with the cops already. I don't need to go through it with you. Everybody knows that retard Stevie took Polly." She glared at Melissa. "He probably got the key from your house. You let him hang around all the time like he's family or something."

Melissa flinched. "The key is right where it has always been. And you know Stevie wouldn't do that. He's family. We're the only family he has."

Presley's eyebrows reared up in skepticism. "You sure about that, Miss Goodie-Two-Shoes? They won't let him play with the kids at the day care center no more cause of what he did. Maybe you'd better get your facts straight."

Jonathan exchanged a look with Melissa. Had he missed something?

Melissa shook her head, weariness and worry heavy in her eyes. "That was a misunderstanding. Stevie was a volunteer. The kids loved him. That one little girl was new. She didn't understand Stevie was only playing. Chief Talbot cleared Stevie of any wrongdoing. He doesn't go back to the center because it puts *him* at risk. Not the children."

"Whatever." Presley slinked out of the room.

William heaved a weary sigh. "I'm sorry." He glanced in the direction his wife had disappeared. "She's not herself."

"A missing child is the sort of nightmare no parent ever wants to go through," Jonathan said, acknowledging the difficulty of the situation. "We all show our pain in different ways."

As if he'd said the words about their situation Melissa turned to him, her gaze searching his.

An old familiar pang ached through Jonathan. He banished the ache and focused on the questions he needed to ask. "The windows are open," he said to William. "Were they open that night?"

William shook his head. "That night it was cold for May. One of those dogwood winters the old timers talk about."

"May I see her room?" Jonathan couldn't name what he was looking for but he needed to get a feel for the family life. He'd formed a pretty strong opinion already and it wasn't good. With William away serving his country most of the time, it didn't appear that anyone was watching after the child in any significant and consistent manner. He felt confident that Melissa did all she could, but he doubted that Presley allowed her interference often.

With visible effort, William nodded and pushed to his feet. "It's, uh, this way."

Jonathan waited for Melissa to go ahead of him but she hesitated. "She knows something." Melissa checked to ensure her brother was well out of hearing. "Something she's afraid to tell."

He didn't have to ask whom she meant. Her sister-in-law. The pain on Melissa's face even as she voiced what Jonathan himself sensed with little doubt made his gut clench. "I agree."

Melissa turned to lead the way to the child's bedroom without saying more, but the relief Jonathan had noted on her face at his agreement made him wonder just how bad a mother Presley had been. Maybe not that bad, he amended. Melissa would never overlook abuse or neglect.

The small house had two bedrooms separated by a bathroom down a short hall from the main living area. The child's room was a little tidier than the rest of the house he'd seen so far. The bed was unmade, stuffed animals lined shelves and themed curtains dressed the windows. The signs of a forensic tech's work remained visible. The room had been dusted for prints and the bed linens had been removed for collection of trace evidence. That last part surprised Jonathan. The official report had shown no indication that sexual abuse was suspected.

Jonathan checked the window. It was closed and locked, presumably the way it was the night the child went missing. The pink paint around the window looked clean and undamaged. The curtains showed no tears.

There was nothing about the room that appeared out of place to an outside observer. Jonathan turned to William. "Does Presley work outside the home?"

"Sometimes she helps out at the diner downtown."

"Who takes care of Polly when her mother works?"

"She goes to the day care center at the First Baptist Church." William's gaze stayed on the child's pillow as he spoke. "It's kind of a mother's day out program. Polly likes going there."

Jonathan wanted to ask about the guy who had harassed Presley, but he would get that information from Melissa later. "Are there any other places Polly goes regularly? Any friends she plays with who live nearby? Any neighbors who were home the night she went missing?" The street was lined on both sides with small homes. Not more than a dozen feet separated them. The police had interviewed neighbors and those who had regular access to the child. He'd read those interviews, as well. Jonathan's strategy would duplicate a lot of that ground. But sometimes the same question asked twice reaped different answers.

"She goes to church with me on Sundays," Melissa

said before William could. "The same church where she goes to mother's day out."

Melissa had gone to church when they were together, Jonathan recalled. He wasn't surprised that she did still. "Any children she plays with regularly? Other parents who are friends of yours, or Presley's?" he asked William.

"The kids next door once in a while," William said, "but not really anyone else outside the kids in the church program."

"Was anyone home that night at the neighbors on either side?" According to the police report the neighbors had been home, but no one heard or saw anything.

William nodded. "Most were already in bed. The police canvassed the entire street. No one remembered hearing anything that night."

"Do you remember what time you left?" The time stated in the report was midnight, which provided a reasonable explanation for no one having been in a position to see or hear any comings and goings.

"A little after midnight." He scrubbed a hand over his face. "It was late. I tried to reason with her, but she insisted I leave."

Not midnight. *After* midnight. "You're sure about the time?"

"Maybe. I guess. I was too angry to really notice. But it was around twelve-thirty when I got home."

"By home," Jonathan clarified, "you mean the

house where you and Melissa grew up?" Where Melissa lived now.

William nodded.

Melissa walked to the window and peered out. This was hard for her, too. She wanted to protect William and Presley, but who was going to protect her?

Who had protected her when he'd walked out on her?

Clearing the past from his head yet again, he asked, "Has Polly ever gotten out of the house or unlocked the door for anyone?" Jonathan couldn't see that being the case at such a late hour, but it wasn't impossible.

William shook his head. "Polly doesn't take to strangers. She'd never leave the house alone or open the door for anyone."

"Never," Melissa confirmed, turning back to the conversation. "She's a sweet child and plays well with the other kids, but she's a little shy around adults that she doesn't know."

Under the circumstances, Jonathan felt there could be little doubt that the child's disappearance was foul play. The only questions were how the person got in and why no one, the mother in particular, heard anything. At least one door had to have been left unlocked.

"Presley didn't unlock the door for any reason after you left?" Jonathan pressed. "And no one was allowed in the house?"

William stared at the floor. "She says she went straight to bed and no one called or came over."

That he didn't meet Jonathan's gaze as he spoke greatly discredited his words and concurrently alluded to what he wasn't saying.

"Does Presley have a habit of hosting company at late hours or leaving the house while Polly is sleeping?"

William met his gaze then. "I can't say for sure. She swears not, but," he shook his head, "she's lied to me before."

"We think she may have left the house that night," Melissa said, visibly struggling with the fact. "After William was already gone. But it couldn't have been for long. She loves Polly too much to take chances like that."

It was wrong and crazy as hell. But Jonathan knew it happened. "She won't admit as much?" He knew the answer before he asked but he needed confirmation.

William shook his head again. "She's sticking to her story that she went to bed and didn't wake up until I came in the next morning."

Pounding echoed through the house, waylaying Jonathan's next question.

"I should get that…" William gestured toward the door. "I'm pretty sure Presley doesn't want to talk to anyone else right now."

"We have other aspects of the case to look into,"

Jonathan offered. "We'll get out of your way for now."

William nodded and went to answer the door.

Jonathan hung back, letting the others go before him. He took one last lingering look at the child's room. Afraid of strangers. Possibly left at home alone. No signs of forced entry or struggle.

Polly was taken by someone she knew. Or she remained asleep during the abduction.

Jonathan's money was on the former.

By the time he reached the living room, William had opened the door to an older man.

"William, what's going on here?" The man looked past William to Jonathan. "Who is this?"

Melissa stepped forward. "Chief, this is Jonathan Foley, a friend of mine."

Jonathan knew all about Chief Reed Talbot, having read a lengthy profile on the man. The chief glared at Melissa, then at Jonathan. "Presley called all upset about some stranger interrogating her about Polly's disappearance."

Jonathan thrust out his hand. "Jonathan Foley. I apologize for not making your office my first stop, but I wasn't sure you'd be available under the circumstances."

Talbot's gaze narrowed with suspicion. "I've been heading the search for Polly. That's where I should be now." He tossed this statement, chock-full of accusation, at Melissa.

"I don't want to get in your way, Chief," Jonathan

insisted. "I'm just here to provide any support I can to a friend."

"Then I'm sure you'll want to hear the news I've come to pass along."

Melissa's breath caught. William's eyes widened with hope.

"We've learned Stevie Price's whereabouts," the chief announced in a rather flat tone.

"Is Polly with him?" Melissa asked, her voice scarcely a whisper.

The chief shook his head. "No, but at least this latest break clears up that question. An eye witness saw Stevie board a bus for Nashville that left early in the evening. Well before the child went missing."

Jonathan recalled reading that a local had gone missing the same day as the child. A local who not only knew Polly but who played with her frequently.

The confirmation that the child wasn't with that missing local opened up the possibility that she was with a stranger. But Jonathan's instincts still leaned toward an intimate—someone the child knew well.

*If* she was still alive.

# Chapter Four

"I may have gone too far." Harry Shepherd dropped his face into his hands. His heart ached with agony. "What have I done?"

Carol Talbot got down on her knees in front of him. "Harry." She took his face in her hands and drew his gaze to hers. "You did the only thing you could."

He wanted to believe she was right. Her eyes shone with the same pain he felt, but also a hope he couldn't quite feel. They were in this together. She'd made a pact with him to do whatever needed to be done… and no looking back. Dear God. He pulled her into his arms. He'd needed someone for so long.

So very long.

This necessary horror had brought them even closer.

"You're right." He kissed her cheek. "It was the only way." As painful as it was, in the end his actions would make everything all right again. The ends justified the means.

He'd worried himself sick for all these months. When William had gotten orders to deploy to Afghanistan, Harry had almost lost his mind. He couldn't watch this happen again. Once in a lifetime was more than enough. He'd had to come up with a plan.

Carol pulled far enough away to look into his eyes once more. She caressed his jaw with the pad of her thumb. "You don't have to worry. Stevie will protect her with his life." The promise of a smile tugged at the corners of her mouth. "This will all be over soon. William will be safe and, if he ever learns the truth, he'll be thankful for the intervention once the initial shock has passed."

Harry wasn't so sure about that, but what the boy didn't know wouldn't hurt him. Keeping the awful details secret would be the best way. Harry closed his eyes. He couldn't love that boy more if he were his own son. *Should have been his son*. Harry shook off the heart-wrenching feelings. That had been a long time ago.

Another lifetime ago.

"As long as it keeps him away from that terrible place," Harry agreed, "that's all that matters." He reminded himself of that fact every hour of every day. Without this intervention William might have perished just as his father had.

Carol moved up to sit on Harry's knee. He smiled

in spite of the misery twisting his soul…in spite of the terrible reality of what he'd done. Doubt nudged his determination once more. *Dear God, please let this be the right decision.*

"Having that no good bum recall seeing Stevie get on that bus was a stroke of genius." She hugged Harry tightly. "You're so smart. Reed didn't suspect a thing. He swallowed the story as easily as he does that homemade cherry pie of mine."

Something else Harry wasn't so sure of. "I would've thought the chief would assume Stevie had taken the bus when the salesclerk came forward to say that Stevie had bought a bus ticket to Nashville." Harry had planned this out very carefully. He'd instructed Stevie to buy that ticket two days in advance of setting this strategy in motion. But Reed Talbot had kept digging until Harry had had to come up with a way to provide confirmation.

Stevie Price had been fascinated with Nashville and country music since he was a kid. Playing guitar was his passion, and he was pretty damned good at it. No one ever believed the mentally challenged man would actually attempt following that dream. It had made complete sense to Harry to go with that idea. Most of the folks in the community didn't care one way or the other about Stevie. Plenty of them were glad he was gone, for whatever reason.

Harry hadn't expected the chief of police to push for finding a witness who'd actually seen Stevie get on the bus. The driver had insisted he couldn't recall any specific passengers. Too many faces, he'd said. Harry had had to step in and pay that drunken fool Floyd Harper to say he'd seen Stevie get on the bus after begging him for a few dollars to buy a bottle of the rot-gut he preferred. Considering Harper's reputation, Harry hadn't been sure the sham would work. Evidently adding the part about his begging for the booze money did the trick.

Apparently it had. The chief had called Harry not twenty minutes ago to confirm that Stevie was in the clear for now. The Nashville police had been notified to keep an eye out for him, but the search for Polly couldn't wait for confirmation of Stevie's whereabouts. The investigation had to move forward under the assumption that Stevie wasn't actually missing in a criminal or legal sense and obviously wasn't involved in Polly's disappearance. That was the chief's position unless Nashville PD called with conflicting information.

After the call, Harry had felt as if a massive boulder had been lifted from his chest. Yet he still couldn't draw a deep enough breath. No matter that the little ruse had worked, this nightmare was far from over.

"What about that man?" Carol asked, worry showing through the courageous face she'd no doubt kept in place just for Harry. "Jonathan Foley? Will he be trouble, you think?"

Harry wished he knew. "Melissa has never said much about him. She'd seemed pretty broken up when their relationship ended a few years back. It's hard to say." Harry exhaled a heavy breath. "What I do know is that Foley's got far-reaching connections in the military, which Melissa believes will help Will." Harry's niece had done the one thing she felt she could to help her brother. But Harry's gut had tied in knots this morning when she'd told him about the step she'd taken.

He was trying hard to give the idea the benefit of the doubt and not to borrow trouble.

This Jonathan Foley could be a godsend.

As long as he didn't sniff around and get a whiff of the truth.

That would destroy the family. And Harry couldn't bear that.

Mercy, what had he done?

Sinners!

Scott Rayburn gritted his teeth as the disgust roiled in his belly. Harry Shepherd and Carol Talbot stood on her porch and hugged.

Scott shook his head. Did they have no shame? What if the chief arrived to find another man on his porch, hugging his wife?

Something was going on between these two. Scott had suspected as much for months now. Bay Minette was a small town. Folks had keenly honed eyes and ears and wagging tongues. He wasn't the only one who'd noticed the looks these two shared whenever they bumped into each other in town.

"Adulterers," he muttered. Scott wished the chief would come home right now. That he would put Harry Shepherd in his place. The man had lorded over his family all these years as if no one in Bay Minette was good enough to get close to a Shepherd.

Fury simmered in Scott's veins. They weren't even Harry's family. But he'd sure as hell stepped in like they were as soon as his little brother was shipped home in a box by the military.

All these years, old Harry had remained unmarried and completely devoted to his dead brother's wife and children. Then she had died and Harry had turned his attention to another man's wife—only the chief wasn't dead. The missing child had evidently given these two the nerve to flaunt their illicit affair a little more flagrantly.

Scott rolled his eyes. Either that or they were up to something more than tawdry behavior. He wouldn't put this whole charade past the two of them to distract folks from their adulterous affair. Could be Harry's attempt to rescue his nephew from going back to that godforsaken place the military had sent him.

No. That couldn't possibly be right. Old Harry worshiped William and his sister, but he loved that little girl even more. He wouldn't dare risk her safety in an outlandish plot such as this.

As boring as the concept was, Scott felt confident the child's disappearance was about her no-good momma. That Presley was a worthless slut. Knowing her, she'd taken the kid off into the woods and left her, hoping she'd never find her way home. God knew Presley showed no real motherly feelings toward the child, much less wifely feelings for her fine husband.

Scott's teeth set hard enough to crack the high priced enamel of the crowns he'd lavished his daddy's money on. William deserved a whole lot better than that worthless woman. But some men were stupid like that. Let a woman use and abuse them. For what? An heir?

Adoption was far less painful.

Carol Talbot, the chief's cheating wife, patted her lover on the back. Scott's lips curled in disgust. Sickening.

The chief had better get on the stick with his retirement. If he kept hanging around Bay Minette he was going to end up retiring alone. He would be rambling around in that big luxury cabin he'd built in Gatlinburg all by himself. What retired couple needed such an enormous home? But nothing would do for his cheating wife but to have the very finest. Far away from the sweltering heat of southern Alabama.

Actually, Scott was in no hurry to see the chief go. The deputy slated to step into his position was about as worthless as a hung jury. With the older generation like Reed Talbot retiring, those Scott's age were stepping into positions of power.

Anticipation trickled into his veins. He couldn't wait for old Judge Baker to retire…or die. Scott was the top attorney in town. Between his stellar reputation and his daddy's money, he was a shoe-in for the judgeship.

Scott slid down in his seat as Harry Shepherd drove past. Scott had parked at the corner of the block just beyond the Talbot home, but he wasn't taking any chances. Harry might be crazier than Scott knew.

When the coast was clear, Scott started his car and eased out onto the cross street. He had a client coming. A wife who'd worked up the nerve to divorce her husband. Poor slob. He had no idea.

As an attorney, Scott knew all about trickery and surprise attacks. But if dear old Uncle Harry was pulling a fast one on William, Scott intended to find out. William deserved the truth.

The chief of police had better get this investigation moving. The longer it took to find the child, the more William would suffer.

Scott considered the outsider Melissa had called in. Maybe this Jonathan Foley would prove more useful than the chief, who was clearly blind. Scott pursed his lips. Somehow he had to ensure that this Mr. Foley had all the facts. No one else would tell him the whole truth the way Scott would. He would have to make that happen, as soon as possible.

That child had to be found.

It was the only way to make William happy again.

And Scott would do anything to see him happy.

He couldn't just sit around here and wait for the chief to get the job done. Every minute that William agonized was one that Scott suffered, as well.

Whether he slept or ate or kept all his appointments or not, Scott intended to ensure the job was done.

Then William would know that there was no one he could count on the way he could count on Scott.

Scott would be a hero.

## Chapter Five

*1:00 p.m.*

William refused to talk to Melissa now. She shouldn't have pushed the issue of Jonathan questioning Presley right away. They hadn't learned anything new and now Presley was even more upset—which made William all the more miserable. Jonathan had kept quiet while Melissa and William argued about Presley's story. She was leaving something out. Something she was too afraid to tell. Melissa wished she could make her understand that if whatever she was holding back helped find Polly, then nothing else mattered. But Presley hadn't been raised in a safe, nurturing home environment. More like a dog eat dog world where only the most cunning survived.

Melissa shifted in the seat of her car and studied Jonathan's profile. What was he thinking? That her family was a little messed up? Probably. Melissa rested her head back against the seat.

"Arguing with your brother isn't going to make

his wife confess to whatever wrongdoing she's committed."

Melissa turned to the driver once more. She wasn't surprised that he'd read her mind. It didn't take ESP to know exactly what she'd been thinking. She shifted her attention back to the street in front of them. "Whatever happened that night was a mistake. Presley would never hurt Polly. She's scared and William is terrified. It's easier not to know, even if it's a mistake."

"I wouldn't misread William's long-suffering attitude for blissful ignorance."

The statement hit a nerve. "I know my brother isn't ignorant," she snapped. "I didn't say that." Why was she biting Jonathan's head off? Good grief, she had to get a grip here. "Sorry. I'm just tired." She was. Totally exhausted, and worried sick. Part of her wanted to shake the hell out of both Presley and William. But more than anything she wanted to protect them…and find Polly.

Jonathan braked at an intersection. "Which way now?"

Melissa sat up straighter. "Sorry. Left. Then right on Blossom Street." Jonathan had offered to drive considering the way her hands had been shaking when they'd left William's. Now she had to focus. Of course Jonathan didn't know which way to go. He'd never been to Bay Minette.

Not once during the six months they were together had he visited or even met her family. Obviously he hadn't cared enough for her. More of that agitation churned inside her. It didn't matter now. Their relationship had been over for three years.

Finding Polly was all that mattered now.

"This Johnny Ray," Jonathan began as he made the turn, "is he going to be cooperative?"

"Depends upon his mood," she answered. "Johnny Ray thinks he's God's gift to women. He can be charming when he wants and a total jerk other times. Honestly, I doubt he'll be any help." But they had to try. She doubted that the chief had pushed him for information. Johnny Ray Bruce had been getting away with just about everything in the book—except murder—since he was born.

Johnny Ray was the same age as William, twenty-five. The two had gone to school together. Had even been friends, sort of, at one time. But Johnny Ray preferred breaking hearts to settling down. As a teenager he'd had a knack for trouble—particularly because the chief of police was his uncle and he wasn't worried about the consequences. Accountability had not been one of his strong suits. Thankfully he'd grown out of that part of his bad boy reputation.

Johnny Ray and Presley had a long, volatile history. One that hadn't completely ended with Presley's marriage to William.

Jonathan parked in front of the small house Johnny Ray's parents had left to him. Neither was dead, just moved down to coastal Florida to retire.

"I guess we'll see," Jonathan said before getting out of the car.

Melissa stared at the small white house. A shiny red sports car sat in the drive out front. Johnny Ray worked as a certified nursing assistant at the same hospital where Melissa worked as a registered nurse. Johnny Ray was a kind and charming caregiver at work. It was only his sexual appetite when off duty that he didn't appear to be able to control. Unfortunately his craving for Presley hadn't lessened with age.

Melissa's car door opened, startling her. Jonathan held it open, waiting for her to climb out. "Thank you." When her mind began drifting off into disturbing memories, she stopped it. Focusing on the here and now was absolutely essential.

The air was thick with humidity, the sort they didn't typically endure until late July or August. The idea that Polly might be trapped out in this heat made Melissa shudder despite the sweltering temperature. The child wasn't old enough to understand that staying out of the direct sun was essential in temperatures this extreme. Dehydration was a major concern. Some had speculated that Polly had gotten up in the middle of the night and wandered off. Every neighborhood in town had been searched. The woods, the parks, no place had been overlooked. She hadn't been found.

Or someone had taken her to a place far enough away that she wouldn't be found.

Tracking dogs had failed to pick up on her scent

no matter that local hunters had shown up with their hounds mere hours after word got out that a child was missing. Two days of rain after that had rendered any trace of her scent undetectable.

As much as Melissa didn't want to believe anyone could have taken that sweet child, defeat was crushing in on her now.

The high-pitched whine of the screen door being opened brought Melissa out of her reverie. She heard Jonathan rap on the faded green door, once, twice.

Melissa swiped at the sweat on her brow with the back of her hand. Johnny Ray had to be here. He worked eight to five most days, but today he was not scheduled. She'd called one of her friends and checked.

Jonathan glanced at her, then pounded on the door a third time.

While they waited he surveyed the yard. Melissa started to ask what he was thinking, but the door flew open sharply enough to have shaken loose some of the flaking green paint.

"What?" Johnny Ray demanded, his eyes slitted against the sun's bright light. He stood in the open doorway, his jeans not even fastened and his muscled chest bare, looking from Jonathan to Melissa and back with blatant irritation. That was another thing Johnny Ray Bruce spent most of his spare time on, pumping iron.

"Johnny Ray, I hate to bother you on your day off," Melissa said. Damn it! Why did her voice have to sound shaky? "But it's urgent." She gestured to the man beside her. "This is my friend Jonathan Foley. We need to speak with you."

Jonathan extended his hand; Johnny Ray hesitated, but then gave it a shake. "Johnny Ray Bruce." He smirked. "Guess you already knew that."

"You work at the hospital with Melissa," Jonathan said. The way he said her name made her chest ache with an old, far too familiar tenderness.

Johnny Ray nodded. "That's right." In Melissa's direction he flashed a smile that didn't reach his eyes. "Course, unlike me, she makes the big bucks."

Ignoring his jab, she got to the point. "Jonathan's here to help with the investigation into Polly's disappearance."

Johnny Ray's cocky expression softened a fraction. "They haven't found her yet?"

Melissa shook her head. "We're hoping we can count on your help."

He took another look at Jonathan then shrugged. "Sure. Come on in."

Melissa followed him inside, with Jonathan close behind her. The place smelled of stale cigarette smoke. Beer cans cluttered the coffee table and both end tables.

Johnny Ray cleared off a spot on the couch and took a seat. "Make yourself at home." He gestured to the other available chairs but didn't bother to clear the mess.

Melissa moved a stack of magazines. Her cheeks

burned when she noted that they were the sort that featured unclothed females in lewd positions. Jonathan took the seat beside her.

Johnny Ray lit a cigarette. "What can I do to help?"

He sounded surprisingly amiable. Melissa looked to Jonathan. She knew what she wanted to ask Johnny Ray but getting emotional wouldn't keep him cooperative. Better to leave this to Jonathan.

"Polly's mother, Presley," Jonathan began, "insists that on the night her daughter went missing, she turned in shortly after midnight and her daughter was in her room asleep. She claims she had no company that evening after her husband left."

Johnny Ray flicked ashes onto the wood floor and shrugged. "Those two fight all the time. If I was a betting man, I'd wager Presley drank herself to sleep after Will left. That's her M.O." He turned to Melissa. "Wouldn't you say, Mel?"

Melissa didn't like when he called her that. No one called her that except him. "I imagine we've all done that at one time or another." Presley had more than her share of issues, but she was Melissa's sister-in-law.

"I'm sensing," Jonathan went on, "that Presley isn't being totally up-front about what happened after her husband left. You're wired in to the local grapevine, from what I hear," he added with something that sounded like respect. "Have you heard any rumors to that effect?"

Melissa held her breath. She felt guilty for sitting by while Jonathan talked behind Presley's back, but if it helped find Polly, she would allow it.

And no one was more connected to the rumor mill than Johnny Ray. That was the reason she and Jonathan were here.

Johnny Ray's expression went from relaxed to guarded despite Jonathan's careful wording of the question. He poked his cigarette into a beer can. "I can't say that I'm wired in to anything." He shot Melissa an accusing look. "But I do know that Presley's marriage has been less than the happily-ever-after she'd expected. Will just can't seem to make her happy." Johnny Ray shrugged. "Sometimes wives seek out that missing happiness in other places."

Rage blasted Melissa. As if he'd felt the detonation, Jonathan put a hand on her arm.

"Are you implying that Presley is having an affair?" Jonathan ventured.

Melissa wanted to be equally angry with Jonathan for voicing the question, but time was slipping away. Painful questions had to be asked. Johnny Ray was the person to ask. He and Presley had carried on a love-hate relationship since she was fourteen. If she had gone that far, chances were the man who'd filled the room with unpleasant secondhand smoke would know.

Johnny Ray executed another of those careless shrugs. "I didn't say that, but I couldn't blame her if she went that route."

This time Melissa couldn't hold back a rebuttal. "William loves Presley. Yes, they have their problems but no marriage is perfect."

Johnny Ray laughed as he lit up another smoke. "I can't argue with that last part."

Melissa bit her lips together. Arguing would be a waste of time, and it might hinder full disclosure. The cockier Johnny Ray felt, the more he'd run off at the mouth.

"So in your opinion her husband hasn't showered her with the attention she deserves. Is that the case?" Jonathan wanted to know.

Melissa glared at him before she could school her expression. How dare he suggest such a thing? William had been deployed for the past six months. That kind of separation strained the best of marriages.

"That's right." Johnny Ray leaned forward and braced his elbows on his knees. "Fact is, she didn't want to have a baby, but Will wouldn't have it any other way. He forced her into going through with the pregnancy and she's been miserable ever since."

No way could Melissa sit here and listen to this. She lunged to her feet. "I need some air."

"Come on, Mel," Johnny Ray said, "you know it's true. She wanted to get rid of the kid and your brother threatened to get a court order to stop her."

Melissa pointed every ounce of rage she felt at the arrogant man. "William had every right to want to save his child. Presley was young and confused—"

"Maybe she couldn't take it anymore," Jonathan

said, cutting Melissa off, "and did what she'd wanted to do all along."

The room filled with silence.

Johnny Ray didn't even blink beneath the weight of Jonathan's stare.

The utter emptiness left by the silence held Melissa in a chokehold.

Presley loved Polly. Melissa would not even entertain such a notion. The idea was unconscionable, downright crazy.

"I'm not saying she did or didn't," Johnny Ray announced, shattering the silence first. "I'm just pointing out that everyone has their limits. Maybe Presley reached hers and made a mistake."

Defeat sucked the anger and certainty right out of Melissa, left her swaying on her feet.

He was right.

Damn it. Johnny Ray knew Presley better than her own husband did, and the point he'd made was frighteningly correct. She hadn't wanted a child. But that was before they'd all fallen in love with Polly, Presley included.

"Johnny Ray, if you know something—"

He held up his hands. "I'm just speculating here, Mel. Laying out some of the facts that some folks don't want to remember."

Jonathan stood, leaned across the cluttered coffee table and offered his hand once more to Johnny Ray. "I hope you'll let us know if you hear anything that might help find that little girl."

Johnny Ray pushed to his feet, gave the out-stretched hand a shake. "Sure thing, man. I'll keep my ears open. No problem."

Melissa swallowed back the crush of emotions swelling her throat. "Thank you." Then she walked out. She couldn't look at him anymore. Not with the ugly truth of his words ringing in her ears.

She didn't stop moving until she was in the car with her seat belt fastened. Her gaze frozen on the street ahead, she couldn't speak as Jonathan started the car and drove away from Johnny Ray's house.

"Is there any possibility he might be right about Presley?" Jonathan asked.

Melissa blinked back the sting of angry tears. Jonathan didn't know her family. His questions were logical and reasonable. She wanted to shake him and make him see that for all her past mistakes and unwise decisions, Presley would never, ever hurt Polly. There were a lot of things about Presley that bothered Melissa. The way she treated William. Her immaturity. But she would not hurt her child. "No." The single syllable echoed in the quiet of the car, the certainty in her tone reaffirming her resolve.

"We need to talk."

"Isn't that what we're doing?" she said, rather than the barrage of excuses on her family's behalf she wanted to offer. She dropped back against the seat, hauled in a deep breath and slowly released it, reminding herself that Jonathan was here to help. She needed to let him.

Jonathan took the next right.

Melissa frowned. "Where're we going?"

"I noticed a cemetery on the way to Bruce's house." Jonathan pulled the car under a massive shade tree that held court over the small parking area that flanked the oldest cemetery in town. "We should have some privacy here."

"Can we walk?" Anxiety and fear were crushing in on her. She didn't wait for his answer. She got out of the car and dragged in a chest full of air. Polly was missing. Possibly dead. Emotion burned Melissa's eyes. It wasn't fair, damn it! She and William had lost their father and their mother. She shot a look at Jonathan as he came around to her side of the car. He'd broken her heart. And now the biggest bright spot in her life was gone. It just wasn't fair!

"I know this is difficult," Jonathan said, his voice soft and understanding.

She didn't want to hear that softness. She wanted him to be strong and do what no one else had—find Polly.

He moved closer and Melissa wanted to back away. She couldn't trust herself with him, not even after all this time. But his eyes—those pale blue eyes she'd dreamed of for so damned long—held her still.

"The police have found nothing. No one is talk-ing." As he spoke his fingers curled around her arms, making her shiver in spite of her determination not to let him see how he affected her. He pressed her with that penetrating gaze. "But I know, just as you do, that someone knows the truth. If we rattle the right cages, that someone will get nervous and make a mistake."

She wanted to fall against him, have those strong arms hold her and those inviting lips promise her that this would be okay. That Polly would be okay. "It can't be Presley. She wouldn't..."

"It's hard. Putting that harsh glare of suspicion on the people you love." He moved closer still, so close she could smell his skin. "But this is the fastest way to get a reaction. There's no time to waste. Too much time has passed as it is."

He was right. A moan rose in Melissa's throat. She had seen the glances exchanged between the policemen working the search. She knew what they thought. Hope was fading.

Melissa couldn't help herself. She fell against Jonathan's chest. His arms went around her and she shuddered with the overwhelming emotions.

"We'll find her," he promised, his lips whispering against her ear. "I won't stop until I do."

Melissa didn't know how he could make such a promise, but somehow she trusted him to be true to his word.

Though she had every reason not to, Melissa believed in Jonathan and the promise he'd just made. He might not be able to commit to a relationship, but she knew enough about his past and his work to know that he would find a way to get the job done. That was the one thing he never failed to do—his job.

She tried to pull herself together, telling herself that as a nurse she faced sickness and death every day at the hospital.

She braced her hands against his chest, resisted the urge to curl her fingers into his shirt and pushed away. She drew in a breath and met his gaze. "What do we do next?" Polly was counting on her. William and Presley were counting on her. Melissa had to be stronger than she'd ever been before. For them.

"The one other person who hasn't been in his or her place since Polly's disappearance is Stevie Price." Jonathan dropped his hands to his sides. "We're going to find out where he really is and what he's up to."

"The chief said he went to Nashville." In truth, she would be the first one to say that she wouldn't have thought Stevie brave enough to attempt to follow that distant dream he'd carried around with him for as long as she could remember. Stevie was only a year older than her. They'd played together as kids, and her family had pretty much taken him in after his folks were gone. He had a good heart, but he just didn't have the mental capacity to pull this off.

Still, she recognized that it wasn't completely impossible.

"The chief could be right," Jonathan acknowledged. "That's what we're going to determine."

She nodded. "Okay. I know Stevie better than most. Where do we start?"

The crunch of tires on gravel drew Melissa's gaze

to the entrance of the cemetery. Will's truck came to a screeching halt next to her car.

Her heart rammed hard against her sternum. Was there news?

Will got out, slammed the truck door hard then stormed in their direction.

The grief she would have seen in his face if there was bad news was absent. Instead, what emanated from his expression and his stiff movements was white hot fury.

William was mad as hell and ready to fight.

# Chapter Six

"She's off limits."

Jonathan kept quiet as Melissa and her brother argued. The pain on her face made Jonathan want to step in and defend her position, but it wasn't his place.

Not anymore.

This was a family matter and he hadn't been anything to Melissa except a bad memory in a very long time.

"I'm not accusing Presley," Melissa repeated, her exasperation showing at this point. She reached out to her brother, but he avoided her touch. The hurt his move generated played out on her face. "You have to see that there's something about that night she's not telling."

William leaned in closer to Melissa, a new blast of fury darkening his face. Jonathan stepped forward. "This isn't going to help us find your daughter."

William glared at Jonathan, his mouth twisted with rage. "You..." He dragged in a shaky breath. "I appreciate what you did for me, Major, but *this* is none of your business. Upsetting Presley was bad enough, but going to Johnny Ray was crossing the line. How do you think that made her feel? She can't take much more."

Jonathan couldn't deny that charge. "You're running on empty, Shepherd." He kept his tone calm and even despite the impatience charging through him. "Fear and frustration are preventing you from seeing the logic in Melissa's words." William started to argue, but Jonathan stopped him with a shake of his head. "Trust me, I know exactly where you are. It's a bad place to be. But alienating the people who care about you because you don't want to see what's right in front of your face is the wrong route to take."

Fury still simmered in William's eyes but he kept his mouth shut.

"I'm sorry, Will." Melissa folded her arms over her chest and lowered her eyes. "I'm not trying to make this any harder. But I'm scared to death that Presley is hiding something that she doesn't realize might help." She lifted her gaze back to her brother's. "Something that might help us find Polly before it's too late."

William swayed back a step. He scrubbed his face with his hands as if he could erase the misery, the confusion. "Presley didn't do anything wrong. It was me. I'm the one who left. I should have been there. But I wasn't and somebody took my little girl."

Melissa pressed her fingers to her trembling lips. She was barely hanging on to her composure. "You couldn't have known." She wrapped her arms around her brother and held him close. "We just have to find the truth and that means asking the hard questions Chief Talbot seems to be avoiding."

Melissa's brother pulled free of her embrace. "Why did you talk to Johnny Ray?" The anger resurrected in Shepherd's eyes. "What does that bastard have to do with anything?"

Melissa glanced at Jonathan. Not for moral support, he suspected. He held up his hands. "I'll take a walk." The two clearly needed some space.

"Johnny Ray keeps up with everybody's business, Presley's in particular. I think maybe he's still stinging that you got the girl he always thought would be his," Melissa was explaining as Jonathan walked away.

Keeping the two in sight, Jonathan moved along the path that skirted the garden of headstones. He needed to clear his head and analyze the meeting with Johnny Ray. The guy had come off as nonchalant. Not quite indifferent but definitely detached. Could be that he could care less about Presley or her child. But based on what Melissa had said about the man's long-running relationship with Presley, his attitude seemed a little too detached.

Jonathan's first thought was that the two had rendezvoused while the child slept—after William Shepherd had departed the home. But there was no evidence of that scenario. Jonathan doubted that either one would admit to having left the child unattended.

There was no reason at this time to consider that Johnny Ray Bruce had anything to do with the child's disappearance. If Polly was the only reason Presley stayed married to Shepherd that could, of course, be considered motive. Yet there was no obvious evidence to that end.

Jonathan stalled. Unless the goal was to do away with the child and then to blame the father. That would get him—as well as the child—out of the picture permanently.

An icy sensation slithered up Jonathan's spine. He hoped like hell that wasn't the case. But there was a ring of clarity to it that unsettled him greatly.

Still, Melissa staunchly stood by the idea that Presley loved her daughter. Was that only what Melissa wanted to see?

"Mr. Foley," a voice whispered from behind Jonathan.

Jonathan shifted to his right, away from Melissa and Shepherd. His muscles tightened in preparation for battle.

"I need to speak to you in private, Mr. Foley."

A man, thirty or so maybe, hovered in the trees that bordered the cemetery on three sides. He leaned to the right and peeked at the couple still debating the subject of Johnny Ray Bruce.

"What about?" It was difficult to dredge up any wariness for a man who crept around in the woods and made contact in such a manner. Particularly one who wore big glasses and a bow tie. But even more surprising was that he'd gotten so close without Jonathan noticing. Definitely not of the norm.

The man nodded toward Melissa and her brother. "Them."

"Who are you?" The guy looked harmless enough. The glasses he wore had inordinately thick lenses. The shirt and bow tie along with the crisply creased trousers didn't really fit with his sneaking around in the woods like this.

The man looked again to see that Melissa and Shepherd were distracted. "My name is Scott Rayburn." He straightened, as if just saying his name out loud called for additional posturing and preening. "There's something you need to know."

Ensuring that Melissa and Shepherd appeared to be discussing their differences calmly, Jonathan moved toward Rayburn. "What is it you have to say?"

"You're not from around here," Rayburn said, seeming nervous with Jonathan's approach. "You don't know these people."

"I know Melissa." Images of her nude body entwined with his made Jonathan flinch.

Rayburn shrugged. "She's blind to what goes on around her."

Jonathan glanced at her, certain this man was incorrect. "I'm reasonably sure she's not as blind as one might think." Just caring. Forgiving. Loving. Passionate. More of those haunting memories whispered through his thoughts, making him weak. He couldn't be weak right now. His jaw clenched. There was never a good time to be weak.

"Perhaps so," Rayburn admitted. "But she's standing by while the rest of her family continues to commit egregious atrocities."

Jonathan's gaze narrowed. What was this guy up to? "Such as?"

"Her uncle is carrying on with the chief's wife while supposedly distraught over William's child."

"Chief Talbot's wife?" Interesting but not necessarily relevant.

Rayburn nodded. "That tawdry affair has been going on for several years now." His head moved from up and down to side to side in a maneuver that made Jonathan think of a bobble head doll. "The chief's as blind as Melissa."

"Does this have anything to do with Polly's disappearance?" Didn't sound that way to Jonathan, but information, however seemingly irrelevant, couldn't be cast aside out of turn.

Rayburn twisted up his courage, or appeared to. "I'm just warning you that you should look into this illicit affair. There's more going on, I believe, than meets the eye."

Jonathan considered the warning. "How can you be certain the chief isn't aware of his wife's extracurricular activities?"

Rayburn covered a grin with one hand. "You really aren't from around here. The chief is completely oblivious to his wife's immorality, just as he is blind to that sorry nephew of his."

Jonathan inclined his head. "Nephew?"

"Johnny Ray Bruce," Rayburn explained. "Presley's lover."

Now they were getting somewhere. "Do you have proof that Presley is still involved with Johnny Ray?" That the man was the chief's nephew might explain why he wasn't under closer scrutiny as a part of the investigation—or at least didn't appear to be. Jonathan had obtained copies of the police reports as well as the witness reports before he'd flown down. Johnny Ray Bruce hadn't been mentioned in any capacity.

"They've never stopped being involved," Rayburn informed him with haughty condescension. "She only married poor Will because his family has a little something and he's likely to make something of himself. Johnny Ray is as lazy as a summer day is long. He's never going to be anything but a worthless bloodsucker."

"Have you spoken to any of the authorities investigating this case? There are others you could tell besides the chief."

Rayburn harrumphed. "The chief is too well known in this area. No one's going to stand up to him, much less tell him his wife is having an affair with the man who used to be his best friend."

Another interesting detail. "Harry Shepherd was once the chief's best friend?"

"That's right." Rayburn preened, attempting to

appear nonchalant as he boasted his great insights. "Played high school football together right here in Bay Minette. Went off to college together. Where you saw one, you saw the other."

"What went wrong?" Again, Jonathan didn't actually see the relevance, but the more information he commanded, the better his ability to analyze.

"Harry's brother, William senior, wanted to serve his country. Harry objected. The chief argued that William senior had a right to follow his own calling. The two have scarcely spoken since."

Melissa had told Jonathan that her father was killed in a military conflict and that her uncle had stepped in to fill his shoes. If this guy's conclusions were correct, Shepherd held the chief's encouragement of his brother against him. Not exactly rational but a reasonable reaction, Jonathan supposed.

"I have to go." Rayburn backed deeper into the tree line. "The police aren't going to look into this," he warned. "Someone needs to."

"What about Stevie Price?" Jonathan asked before Rayburn could creep away. "The chief said he'd taken off to Nashville. Any theories on that one?" Jonathan suspected that Price's disappearance the same night as Polly's was no coincidence.

"Stevie is a mentally handicapped grown man," Rayburn said with glaring disdain. "Folks around here allow him to play with their children as if he's one of them. But he's not." Rayburn pressed Jonathan with an accusation in his gaze. "I say good riddance."

"Do you have proof that Price isn't as harmless as most seem to think?" An uneasiness settled in Jonathan's gut. This guy Price was an unknown variable.

Rayburn snorted. "Ask Mrs. Syler at the day care center. She'll tell you she almost had to get a restraining order to keep him off the playground. He used to go there and play with the kids sometimes." He shook his head. "But not anymore."

The chief hadn't mentioned that in his reports, and Melissa had insisted the incident was a mistake. That Stevie's work as a volunteer was sanctioned by the day care owner. They were going to have to dig a little deeper. Melissa seemed protective of Stevie; then again, she tried to protect all those she cared about. But finding the child trumped all else.

"I have to go now."

Jonathan glanced toward Melissa and Shepherd. As Shepherd climbed into his truck and started the engine, Melissa watched, her arms folded over her chest.

Before Jonathan could ask any more questions, Rayburn disappeared into the woods.

Strange character. Jonathan walked back to where Melissa waited, watching her brother drive away.

"You okay?" Dumb question under the circumstances.

She quickly wiped her eyes. "I guess so. He wants

me to back off where Presley is concerned and—"
she released a heavy breath "—I can't. She's afraid
of something. We have to know what that is."

Understandable. Presley was the last person to see
Polly before she disappeared and was supposedly in
the house when she went missing. That made her the
primary person of interest if not the prime suspect.

"Has Chief Talbot voiced any concerns about Presley?"

Melissa shrugged. "Not really. Until now he's been
solely focused on Stevie."

That was the problem when bad things happened
in small towns. Everyone knew everyone else. Made
objectivity next to impossible.

"What about your uncle?" Jonathan asked as he
ushered her toward the car. "Is there anything going
on with him that we haven't talked about?" He figured
he might as well explore Rayburn's allegations.

Melissa stopped and turned back to him, confusion
cluttering her face. "What do you mean?"

This line of questioning would be more than a
little sensitive. "Your uncle has never married. Is
there a particular reason?" That was about the only
way Jonathan could think to ask about his social life
without asking outright about the rumor he'd just
heard.

"I don't know. He's taken care of William and
me since we were kids back in elementary school.
I guess he never had time to focus on his own life."

Her confusion turned to suspicion. "Why would you ask that?"

He could dance around the question or he could just ask. "Are you aware that there is a rumor that he's carried on a long-term affair with the chief's wife?"

The suspicion morphed into dismay. "Who would say such a hurtful thing?"

"Scott Rayburn." Jonathan wasn't going to hide anything from Melissa. He'd done enough of that in the past. Finding her niece was too important to play games on any level.

"Scott?" Renewed confusion chased away the rest of the emotions playing out in her eyes. "Why on earth would he say something like that? We went to school together. He's come to picnics and family get-togethers at our house for as long as I can remember. He helped Will through physics in high school." She reached into the pocket of her jeans and pulled out her cell phone. "I want him to say that to me."

"Wait." Jonathan put his hand over hers. The contact made his breath catch. She stared up at him as if she'd experienced the same jolt. When he'd recovered, he offered, "It's important that we consider all the possibilities, even the ones that turn out to be rumors. Tell me about Rayburn."

She relaxed a fraction. "He's a little older than me and kind of different from most guys around here."

"Define different," Jonathan suggested.

She shrugged. "This is Alabama. Football is a

religion and hunting is a male rite of passage. Scott preferred reading and *socializing*. He was always more like one of the girls. He went to law school and has his own boutique law firm downtown. Never married. He loves his work too much."

"Do you know of any reason why he would dislike your uncle? Does he have a grudge against your family? Any reason at all that he would spread these kinds of rumors?"

Melissa shook her head. "That's the part that doesn't make sense. My mother always said that actions speak louder than words. Scott has always acted as if he loves us." She rubbed her eyes. "Folks used to insist he had his eye on me, but I never noticed."

When he didn't respond, Melissa glanced around and said, "I guess we should get going."

An intense sensation jabbed Jonathan. He stood very still, denied the feeling, as she walked toward her car.

Jealousy.

He gave himself a swift mental kick. He had no right to be jealous where Melissa was concerned.

A few hours in Melissa's presence and already he was losing his hold on control.

The cell in Jonathan's pocket vibrated. He checked the screen and saw it was an Out of Area number. *The boss.*

"Foley," he announced in greeting.

"Thought I'd let you know that Victor Lennox has agreed to flip on his connections."

Not really news to Jonathan. He'd expected as much. "I suppose that's a good thing." To Jonathan it meant that the man would get off with a slap on the wrists for his crimes.

"Don't worry," his employer said knowingly, "he's not going to get off as easy as you think. Lennox isn't the sort they let walk away."

Jonathan sure hoped not.

"How are things in Alabama?"

The question surprised Jonathan. His employer rarely delved into personal territory on any level. "The child is still missing and the investigation is moving at about the speed of molasses."

"Let me know if you need anything in the way of backup. I stand behind my people on and off the job. You don't need to tread water there or anywhere else."

"Thank you, sir. I'll keep that in mind."

The connection severed.

Jonathan slid the phone back into his pocket. Strange. He'd never worked for an employer whose name he didn't know much less whose face he'd never seen.

Nonetheless, he trusted his instincts and not a single warning had gone off where the man was concerned. He operated this new Equalizers agency with utter discretion and immense compassion.

A man like that couldn't be all bad.

Jonathan joined Melissa in the car. She'd settled

into the passenger seat. Driving wouldn't be in her best interest or anyone else's just now.

For a moment they sat in silence. He didn't want to prod her for answers. She was tired and worried. Jonathan could understand each of those reactions.

"I'm scared, Jonathan."

He turned to her, his chest tight at the sound of her voice. "I know."

"If someone has hurt that baby…" She closed her eyes and held back the emotions making her lips tremble.

He wanted to tell her not to worry, but the truth was, at this point, the possibility that Polly was a victim of some unspeakable violence was extremely high.

"We'll find her," he promised. "And then we'll deal with whatever we have to deal with."

A tear slid down Melissa's cheek. "I've spent my entire adult life taking care of people as a nurse. Helping those who can't care for themselves." She moved her head side to side. "But I swear, if someone hurt that child, I want to hurt them." She compressed her lips and visibly fought for composure. "If she's…" she swallowed with difficulty "…dead…I want whoever is responsible to…" she drew in a jerky breath "…I want them to pay."

# Chapter Seven

*Chicago, 4:00 p.m.*

He sat at a table inside Maggie's Coffee House. The one closest to the window that provided the most direct view of the building across the street.

*The Colby Agency.*

Maggie James swiped at the counter, her attention not on business as it should be. Her entire being was focused on *him*.

Every day he came into her shop and sat from three until six or seven, depending upon when the staff at the Colby Agency left for the day. He stayed, staring like that, until the lights on the fourth floor across the street went out.

Her chest ached as she drew in a ragged breath. She wanted to order him out of her life. For months now she had known this thing between them would come to no good, but she couldn't bring herself to let go. He was an addiction to her. She couldn't sleep if he didn't come by the shop every day. Couldn't breathe if he didn't make love to her almost as often.

Night after night he came to her bed and made love to her as no other man ever had. Then he disappeared into the night, like the fog after a long, hard rain. He'd told her his name was Slade Keaton. That he was thirty. A full two years younger than her. She had no idea where he'd come from or what he'd done before. He was here now, and that was what mattered. That was his stock answer.

*A big mistake, Maggie.*

She forced her attention back to cleaning up after the last of the lunch stragglers. She had worked hard to make something of herself, to make this coffee shop the place to stop for a relaxing break on the Magnificent Mile. Why screw it up now by getting involved with trouble?

She had been asking herself that question for well over six months now. Somehow she never seemed able to dredge up the proper answer. The answer that would put her back on track and out of this crazy spin cycle.

Broad, square hands flattened on the counter she'd just scrubbed. Maggie's breath caught as her gaze lifted and collided with steel gray eyes. She laughed tightly. "You startled me."

That smile that swept away every fiber of her resistance spread across his handsome face. "I'll be back around seven-thirty."

She covertly glanced at the fourth floor of the building across the street. He was leaving before the lights went out? "Seven-thirty?" she asked. It wasn't exactly a clever response, but it was all she had.

"We're going to dinner."

She perked up. "Dinner?" Jeez, she sounded like a canary, repeating everything he said. He so rarely did anything spontaneous, the announcement had anticipation zinging through her.

"That's right." He winked. "Wear that little green dress I like so much."

Her head moved up and down and her lips smiled. She recognized both these things but her heart wouldn't slow down enough for her to respond any other way.

He squeezed her hand.

Then he was gone.

She watched him stride down the sidewalk until he was out of view, then her gaze drifted to the fourth floor across the way.

As if he possessed some sixth sense or ESP or whatever, the lights went out.

The folks at the Colby Agency were going home.

*8:00 p.m.*

VICTORIA COLBY-CAMP placed the linen napkin in her lap as her husband took his seat across from her. He looked more handsome than ever in his navy suit. She loved that color on him.

Incredibly, Lucas Camp had, indeed, retired from his government consulting work. He spent several days per week working alongside her at the Colby Agency. Victoria could not be happier. Having both her husband and her son at the agency with her was a dream come true. Contentment settled deep inside her.

She had waited a long, long time for this level of happiness.

"Wine?" Lucas asked as the waiter approached their table.

"Absolutely."

Lucas ordered the finest house wine. She loved that he knew her so very well. This was her favorite restaurant, and he'd ordered her favorite wine.

When the waiter had moved on, Lucas settled his gaze on her. "Victoria, I have a proposition for you."

She lifted her eyebrows in question. "Sounds intriguing."

"We haven't taken a vacation since our honeymoon." He deftly draped a napkin in his lap. "I'm thinking white sands and sparkling blue waters."

"Ah, Grand Cayman." She'd mentioned never having been there. Once again, her dear husband wanted to please her. But she also knew a place he treasured very much. "How about Puerto Vallarta?"

His knowing gaze narrowed. "Shall we toss a coin?"

"We took a cruise last time," she reminded him.

He nodded. "We'll look into reservations for Mexico then."

The waiter arrived and poured their wine. Lucas thanked him. "Speaking of reservations," he said when they were alone again—if one could be alone in a popular restaurant during the dinner hour. "I presume you have no reservations regarding Jim's ability to handle the agency if we're gone a week or two."

"I do not." Her son had done a spectacular job. The merger between his staff of former Equalizers and her investigators at the agency was now seamless. The final result was a phenomenal team.

"Jim doesn't appear to miss running his own shop," Lucas commented.

"I agree." Jim had sold the brownstone as well as the Equalizers business several months ago. "He's home now, in every respect." Lucas knew how much that meant to her. "I am so grateful."

Lucas reached across the table and patted her hand. "As am I." He inclined his head and looked past Victoria. "Isn't that Maggie?"

Victoria turned to see who'd entered the dining room. The hostess led a handsome couple through the maze of elegantly dressed tables. "Yes, it is Maggie." Maggie James owned and operated the coffee house across the street from the agency. She noticed Victoria and smiled, then waved.

Maggie touched her dinner companion's arm and gestured to Victoria and Lucas's table. The man with

Maggie said something to the hostess, then the two of them made their way over.

"He's quite handsome," Victoria said in an aside to Lucas.

"I'll take your word for that," he murmured back, then stood. "Maggie." Lucas gave her a peck on the cheek.

Maggie literally beamed. "What a coincidence."

"Vinelli's is my favorite restaurant," Victoria said. "If you haven't been here before, you're going to love it."

"Oh." Maggie pressed a hand to her chest. "Forgive me. This is Slade Keaton." She turned to the tall, silent man at her side. "Slade, this is Victoria Colby-Camp and her husband, Lucas."

Slade nodded to Victoria. "It's a pleasure to meet you, Mrs. Colby-Camp."

Lucas extended his hand. "Keaton."

"Mr. Camp."

Maybe it was Victoria's imagination but Maggie's friend seemed slow to take Lucas's hand. Once he did, however, they shook firmly. Maybe she was just tired. They'd had a long week at the agency. Closing up shop a couple of hours early had been the least she could do for her staff.

Victoria studied the man, Slade Keaton, while Maggie and Lucas made small talk. Lucas, she knew, had a soft spot for the hardworking lady. Maggie was utterly charming and quite lovely, with fiery red hair and vibrant green eyes. She and her companion made quite a handsome couple.

Keaton watched Lucas closely as he spoke. Was it a protective instinct toward his lady? Perhaps, Victoria thought. But something about him didn't feel quite right to her.

Keaton suddenly turned his face ever so slightly and smiled at Victoria, as if he'd heard the thought.

*Don't be foolish.* Victoria blamed her suspicions on her state of fatigue. Besides, how was a man supposed to act when introduced to total strangers in the middle of a restaurant when he had obviously come to be seated and served?

"The hostess is waiting," he said to Maggie. To Lucas and Victoria, he said, "Enjoy your meal."

When the two had moved on to their table, Lucas leaned forward. "I think this is the first time I've seen Maggie on a date."

"She works so hard," Victoria agreed. "I'm glad she's taking some time for herself."

Lucas made an agreeable sound, but his attention remained on the couple being seated a few tables away.

Victoria started to ask Lucas if he'd sensed anything odd about the man but decided against it.

Tonight was about relaxing, not dissecting the social life of someone as kind as Maggie James.

Victoria glanced at the man accompanying Maggie once more. He looked directly at her as if he'd felt her gaze on him. A second, then two and three passed before he looked away.

*Odd.*

Victoria banished the idea…but the one thing she had always trusted, besides her husband, of course, was her instincts.

Funny how they were humming just now.

Perhaps it would be in Maggie's best interest if Victoria did a little looking into this Slade Keaton. It wouldn't hurt and Maggie never had to know.

"I know what you're thinking," Lucas said, summoning her from the scheming thoughts.

"I'm certain you don't." Victoria reached for her wine.

"You're thinking," Lucas said, picking up his own glass, "that you might check out Mr. Keaton, just to make sure Maggie isn't getting herself into any trouble."

Victoria tried to keep the guilt out of her expression. It didn't work. *I knew it* flashed in Lucas's eyes. "She's likely quite lonely. A lonely woman is easy prey."

Lucas held up his glass for a toast. "To the most caring and compassionate woman I know."

Victoria blushed and clinked her glass against his. "And one who can be somewhat nosy from time to time."

"Don't worry about Maggie," Lucas assured her. "I'll look into Keaton myself."

"Now who's being nosy?" Victoria laughed. It felt good after the busy week they'd had.

"What can I say?" Lucas enjoyed a long swallow of his wine. "I cut my investigative teeth on the CIA. I can't help myself."

Victoria stole a look at the couple in question. "Well, I hope Mr. Keaton is on the up and up." If he wasn't, he wouldn't be hiding anything for long. No one could hide a single fact from Lucas Camp when he chose to find the whole story.

"We'll soon know."

Victoria relaxed. Maggie was in good hands with Lucas providing backup.

The world needed more men like Lucas Camp.

# Chapter Eight

Where was Harry? Melissa needed him here. He always made the most confusing or troubling situations better.

Melissa paced the length of the living room again. She'd been doing that for hours now. Jonathan had tried to calm her but his reassuring words had not helped.

Floyd Harper was dead. He'd fallen off the overpass on Main Street. It appeared to be an accident, but the chief wouldn't make an official announcement until the forensics work was completed.

That Harper was the only witness to Stevie having left town made his sudden death suspicious.

Chief Talbot had called with word on that awful development an hour ago. He hadn't wanted Melissa to see it on the news or hear it any other way. Already folks were tying it to Polly's disappearance. Calling it murder.

Melissa hugged her middle. Mr. Harper was an

alcoholic, that was all too true. But, to her knowledge, he had never hurt a flea. He lived in an old rundown house trailer on the edge of town and spent most of his days liquored up on whatever he could afford. Yet, he never got into trouble. Never bothered anyone. The only time he'd ever spent a night in jail was the time he'd passed out on a park bench and the chief had insisted he sleep it off in a cell so Harper would remember never to do anything like that again.

How could he have anything to do with Polly's disappearance? The only connection was that Harper had been the one to confirm Stevie had gotten on that bus to Nashville.

Melissa raked her fingers through her hair, massaged her skull in an effort to ease the tension there. This just didn't make sense. Stevie would never hurt Polly. Certainly Mr. Harper wouldn't. How on earth could this be happening?

"Tell me again what happened to Price's family."

She turned to Jonathan when he spoke. He sat on the sofa surrounded by old high school yearbooks and family photos that included Stevie. "His mother abandoned him when he was just a kid and his father passed on years later. His father was another Floyd Harper. He couldn't stay sober, much less take care of a child. Folks around town, my family in particular, picked up his slack. Stevie's parents weren't bad people; they just had a lot of bad breaks."

Jonathan studied several photos that he'd spread

on the coffee table in front of him. "He seems very happy with your family."

Exhausted, Melissa sat down on the sofa next to him. Her pulse sped up with the brush of their shoulders. She'd been reacting that way all day. It was ridiculous but she couldn't suppress her body's reactions. "Stevie has been like a part of the family since he was a kid." The theory that he might have taken Polly didn't make sense. None at all. It was about as farfetched as the idea that Uncle Harry was having an affair with Carol Talbot. Ridiculous.

Yet, deep down Melissa understood that Harry had been very lonely since her mother had passed away and she and William had grown up. But Harry just wasn't the sort of man to do such a thing.

"Tell me about the chief's wife," Jonathan said, as if he'd picked up on Melissa's last thought. He'd always been able to do that. When they were together, she'd accused him of reading her mind too many times to count.

"They've lived here for as long as I can remember. The chief is preparing for retirement. They bought a place in Gatlinburg, Tennessee. They were supposed to leave already but he doesn't want to go until this…" she swallowed hard "…is resolved. His wife has never worked outside the home despite having a degree in education."

That Jonathan wasn't letting go the idea that Harry and Carol were having an affair raised Melissa's hackles. He was right, she realized on an intellectual level, to consider every possibility. Even though this possibility was a waste of time.

"She planned to teach," Melissa explained, "but they wanted children first." She replayed the comments she could recall that her mother had made over the years about the chief and his wife. Most of the ladies in town considered Carol Talbot a bit uppity, but Melissa's mother had always spoken kindly of her. "I think there were several miscarriages before Carol had a successful pregnancy."

Jonathan looked surprised to hear this. "I was under the impression they didn't have children."

"They did," Melissa explained. "Just one. A little girl. She was born when I was about four." Dragging up those awful memories sent another stab of misery deep into her chest. "A beautiful little girl. Like her mother." Carol Talbot was a gorgeous woman. "When she was four she drowned. It was really awful." Melissa shivered, hugged herself again. "I don't know how a person gets over something like that." And she didn't want to know.

"I don't think they do."

Melissa searched Jonathan's face, his eyes. There had always been something he held back from her. That had been part of the problem, she suspected. "You lost someone?" He wouldn't tell her. She'd asked that question before, but he'd never elaborated on the shadow that hung over his past. They talked about his history to a point, but there was always that place he avoided.

"You could say that."

And that was as far into his past as Jonathan Foley ever allowed her. It shouldn't bother her all these years later, but somehow it did.

Jonathan turned his attention back to the photos again. "That's why the chief isn't retiring as planned."

"Yes. He won't leave without finding Polly." The chief wouldn't leave this investigation up to anyone else. He knew every citizen in this town, some since birth. He wasn't going anywhere until this was done. Melissa appreciated his loyalty. Calling Jonathan for help was no reflection on the chief's determination to solve the case. He had gone above and beyond. And he'd found nothing. Chief Talbot could use all the help he could get, whether he wanted it or not.

In truth, it was that close-knit relationship between the chief and the citizens he protected that worried Melissa. She couldn't imagine anyone in town being responsible for Polly's disappearance. Would the chief's training and years of experience help him to see beyond what he thought he knew to be true?

"Sometimes," Jonathan began, "in their grief, people go to extremes they wouldn't have gone to before to assuage the pain."

"Like having affairs." Melissa knew where he was going with this. "I just can't see Carol or Harry doing something like that. He and the chief have been friends for most of their lives. They played football together in high school. Harry was the chief's best man at his and Carol's wedding." Melissa hadn't been born yet, but she'd heard all the stories, seen the photos.

"Rayburn suggested your uncle and the chief haven't spoken in years."

A frown furrowed across Melissa's brow. What was Scott up to? He loved stirring trouble, thrived on drama. He never hurt anyone, just kept small-town life interesting. But this was a missing child. Polly, for God's sake. Setting her frustration aside, she weighed the comment he'd made to Jonathan. "Uncle Harry was always too busy taking care of us to have much of a social life."

Melissa tried to think of a time when she'd seen him and the chief together—in any setting—carrying on a conversation. Surely she had. Yet, strangely, she couldn't recall even one. Scott could very well be putting one and two together and coming up with four. Just because the chief and Harry were busy didn't mean they weren't friends anymore. And just because Carol had suffered an agonizing loss didn't make her an adulteress.

Still, Melissa recognized that Jonathan had a point. "Carol Talbot shops." Those same ladies in town who didn't care for Carol whispered behind their hands about her outrageous shopping sprees. "She goes on big shopping trips, sometimes all the way to New York. She wears only the best. Her home is decorated equally beautifully." Melissa shrugged. "I guess buying things became her distraction."

"Sometimes a distraction works for a while,"

Jonathan put forward, "then that person needs something more. Like a drug addiction. When the same old drug doesn't do the trick anymore, it takes something new and stronger, more daring than the last."

He was preaching to the choir. As a nurse, Melissa understood the human psyche. She shook her head. "Maybe. But not with my uncle. He's not that kind of man. He'd never do that to the chief." Harry had been like a father to her and to William. He'd sacrificed any thoughts of having his own family to take care of his younger brother's. A man like that didn't get involved with another man's wife. He wouldn't be that selfish. Melissa refused to believe that for a moment.

"According to Rayburn," Jonathan said, despite her wish that he would forget about Scott, "Stevie's fascination with the children in the community is trouble waiting to happen. Is there any possibility that he has inappropriate feelings for any of the children? Have you watched his interactions closely enough to truly judge that aspect? I'd like you to put your feelings for the man aside. Is it possible?"

Melissa rose and started pacing again. She didn't want to think of Stevie in that way. He wasn't really a man, in that sense. He was a child. Why did someone always have to make every little thing bad? She hated that. "I played with him myself growing up." She shook her head adamantly. "Stevie doesn't think that way. I'm as sure of it as I am of anything."

"But you were both kids then," Jonathan reminded

her. "What about now? Physically, Stevie's a man. Think, Melissa." He pressed her with that deep, deep, penetrating gaze that still haunted her dreams. "Are you absolutely certain Rayburn is wrong?"

Hesitation and confusion muddied her thinking process. "I don't know." She turned away from him and walked to the window. It was dark outside. Nothing to stare at but the moon. "I guess it's not completely impossible." She looked over her shoulder at Jonathan. "But I've never witnessed anything untoward in Stevie's behavior in any setting with anyone." That was the truth. She would stand by that until solid evidence proved otherwise.

And if she was wrong...

*Don't let him have started with Polly.*

*Not Polly.*

Jonathan joined her at the window. "You don't want to consider this line of thinking," he said quietly. "But Harper was the one witness who could place Stevie on that bus and now he's dead. Stevie has deep affection for Polly and the two went missing the same day. That can't be coincidence, Melissa. No matter how you look at it—no matter what you think you know—the facts speak for themselves."

She closed her eyes, held back the emotions that threatened. He was right. She couldn't deny his words any longer. After all her family had done for Stevie, surely he wouldn't have hurt Polly. Yet, on an intellectual level, she knew those very things happened.

Not to her family…they'd suffered enough already.

"Tomorrow," Jonathan said gently, "we'll confront Rayburn together. I'm certain there is more he didn't tell me. He seems like the type who won't want to be one-upped. If you refute his claims, he may spill more than he intends in order to prove you wrong. Any information we gain from him could prove useful."

She nodded. "I can do that." Scott loved being right. And most of the time he was. Just not this time.

Headlights flashed across the window, then extinguished. Melissa peered through the darkness to determine who had arrived. Her heart rate kicked into a faster rhythm. Harry.

"It's my uncle." She turned to Jonathan. "Maybe I should talk to him alone." Harry hadn't seemed as enthusiastic about her call to Jonathan as she'd hoped he would be. If she intended to ask him any sensitive questions, he would be most unhappy if she did so in front of Jonathan.

"I have some calls to make." Jonathan stepped away from the window. "I'll be out back if you need me."

Melissa resisted the urge to launch into his arms and go with him. She didn't want to think about these questions, much less ask them. And she was tired. So very tired. She closed her eyes and banished the images of sweet little Polly out there somewhere, alone in the dark.

Or worse.

Melissa shuddered. She had to keep herself strong. Polly needed her.

The front door opened and Harry stepped inside. He didn't live here but he might as well have. He'd been a part of this family in every sense of the word for Melissa's entire life.

Their gazes collided. "Hey." She couldn't manage a respectable smile for him, but she tried to infuse hope into her expression. The grim set of his made her heart pound harder. Surely there wasn't more bad news.

"I need to talk to you, Melissa."

Fear skittered through her veins. "Is there news?" *Please, please don't let it be bad.*

Harry trudged over to a chair and dropped into it. He was showing every day of his fifty-eight years tonight. They were all showing signs of sheer exhaustion and overwhelming misery.

She sat down on the sofa and clasped her hands in her lap to prevent them from shaking. "What's wrong?"

"William is beside himself." Harry swiped a hand over his face. "He's torn up over the idea that you and your friend believe Presley had something to do with Polly's disappearance."

Melissa hated that Harry and William were hurt by Jonathan's questions, but they had to be asked. She had come to terms with that painful fact. Presley was hiding something. There was no doubt in Melissa's mind.

"I know Presley would never purposely do anything to hurt Polly," Melissa explained. "But William's got to see that something's wrong with her story. She's hiding something. Whatever she's leaving out might be relevant in a way she doesn't understand."

"I can't deny that likelihood." Harry slumped back into the chair. "But, good God, girl, she's William's wife. You can't expect him not to be hurt by those kinds of allegations."

Melissa's guilt for hurting her brother or Presley gave way to frustration. "I'm sorry as I can be that either of them is hurt by this, Uncle Harry, but Polly is missing." Melissa lifted her hands, turned her palms upward in question. "She's been gone almost six days. We can't afford to take the chance that there's some aspect of the circumstances of that night that isn't being considered. Those of us closest to Polly have to double the scrutiny on every step we made before her disappearance."

Harry lowered his head and gave it a shake. "You're right, of course." He heaved a burdened breath and met Melissa's gaze once more. "But it's so hard to watch him suffer like this."

Melissa got up and walked over to kneel down in front of her weary uncle. "I know." She reached her arms around his neck and hugged him close. "We'll get through this. Momma always said the Shepherds were made of strong stock. We can do what has to be done."

Harry hugged her close. "We will. I promise you that. We will *all* get through this."

Melissa closed her eyes and inhaled deeply, drawing in the familiar, comforting scent of the man who had been more father than uncle to her. He patted her back, murmured reassuring words.

She stilled as she sniffed another scent on his collar. A cloying smell that overpowered his usual herb-scented aftershave. Melissa analyzed the sweet fragrance. Perfume. She vaguely recognized the expensive designer brand.

Where had she smelled that perfume before?

Carol Talbot.

The air exited her lungs in a whoosh.

All the reasons why that scent might be clinging to her uncle's shirt filtered through her, ramming against the logic that could not be denied. He may have bumped into Carol that evening. She might have hugged him in deference to this nightmare in which the whole family was trapped. He might have…

*Don't be stupid, Melissa.*

There had to be a reasonable explanation for the dose of Carol's perfume that permeated her uncle's shirt. A good, long hug under current circumstances wasn't outside the realm of possibility. And just because Carol was the only woman Melissa knew who wore that particular perfume didn't mean there weren't others. Maybe.

Melissa drew back, propped a smile in place. "You're right. We'll find Polly safe and sound and everything will be all right."

"No question." Emotion shimmered in his eyes. "You have my word on that. The whole family will be all right. I promise."

She nodded, couldn't bring herself to speak. He was so sure. He'd always taken such good care of Melissa and her brother. His confidence now heartened her, despite Scott Rayburn's accusation echoing in her brain.

"I know your friend is trying to help," Harry said. "Nothing I could say or do would ever be thanks enough for what he did for William, getting those orders delayed. Maybe if he could just go a little easy on William and Presley it would be better."

"I'll talk to him." Melissa got to her feet and backed away a step. Carol Talbot's preferred scent haunted her senses. There had to be an explanation. *There just had to be*.

Harry stood. "Get some rest. I'm going back out on the search tomorrow morning."

Melissa nodded. "I'll be there, too."

She walked her uncle to the door and said goodnight, her head reeling with questions.

Could she really have been that blind all these years? Harry Shepherd had always been a hero to her, the man she could call upon for anything at any time. The idea of him having an affair with his best friend's wife...well, it just didn't make sense.

Melissa took a deep breath, pushed that worry away and went in search of Jonathan. She wasn't ready to admit Scott Rayburn might be right—not until she had more solid proof. If Harry was having an affair with Carol, it had nothing to do with the search for Polly.

Jonathan leaned against a porch post, staring out into the night. The big moths flying around the glow of the overhead light sent fluttering shadows over his tall frame.

"My uncle's gone now."

Jonathan turned to her. "Is there news?"

Melissa shook her head. She folded her arms over her chest and moved up beside Jonathan. "He's worried about William. He asked if you could go a little easier on Presley next time you speak to her."

Jonathan resumed staring out into the darkness. "Even if doing so stonewalls finding the child?"

Melissa's belly cramped with agony. "He didn't mean that. He's just worried about William. And Polly," she added to ensure Jonathan got it. She thought of all the times she and William had depended on Harry and he'd never let them down. "He's certain we'll find her and that everything will be all right again." That part bothered her a little for some reason. He was so sure. Maybe he just wanted to give Melissa more confidence. That would be just like him. He'd done the same thing when she'd tried out for the girls' volleyball team in high school. He'd sworn she would make the team. And she had.

To this day she wondered if he'd put a bug in the coach's ear.

Jonathan turned to stare at her, his doubt set in grim lines on his face. "I heard that part."

Melissa's jaw dropped in surprise. "You were listening to our conversation?"

Jonathan held her gaze, his expression unflinching. "He's very confident considering this investigation has gone nowhere and the child has been missing for nearly a week." He turned to face her fully. "There's something you need to understand."

She braced for the words to come. Judging by the unyielding look in his eyes, whatever he had to say was going to hurt.

"There's no evidence. No ransom demand. Nothing."

Each word was like a spear sliding through her chest.

"The chances of finding that child alive after almost a week are slim to none."

She opened her mouth to rail at him but he stopped her with a raised hand. "Unless," he qualified, "the person who abducted her is someone she knows. Someone who has an ulterior motive for keeping her hidden away. And safe. If the motive for taking her is not for money or some perverted pleasure, there has to be another reason."

Melissa's eyes widened with the disbelief pounding against her sternum. "You're accusing William or Harry, aren't you?"

He shrugged. "Maybe Presley."

"That's crazy." Melissa wasn't buying that. She twisted away from his hard gaze, refused to be swayed by the conviction on his face, in his tone.

"Four people have something to gain by William's deployment orders being changed," Jonathan went on, the truth in his words like salt in her aching wounds. "William, Harry, Presley and you."

Melissa whirled toward him once more. "Now you're accusing me?"

"I'm merely pointing out that the four of you have motive. That is what the chief should have looked at first. Considering the lack of a ransom demand, who had the most to gain by her going missing? It's a hard question, Melissa, but it needs to be asked. If Talbot isn't asking, he's making a mistake. No matter how well he knows you and your family."

She lifted her chin and glared at him. "I'm not discussing these ridiculous accusations with you another moment."

"I'm not suggesting," he offered with a calmness that infuriated her all the more, "that your uncle or your brother or his wife did any harm to the child—"

"Polly," Melissa corrected. No way was he getting away with making her a case statistic or mere victim. She was Polly. Pain sheared through Melissa again. "Her name is Polly."

"Polly," he acknowledged. "I don't believe harm to Polly was intended. But what I do believe is that one or all three knows far more than they're telling. Until we know all the facts, we're wasting our time."

Melissa had had enough of this. "Fine. Tomorrow morning we'll have a family meeting. You can present your suspicions and no one will leave the room until you're convinced that we're all innocent. I'll lock the doors." Fury squeezed out the pain radiating inside her. She wasn't afraid to put any member of her family on the spot. Not one of them would do this. The idea was ludicrous.

"Melissa."

That she melted a little at the way he said her name made her all the angrier. "Don't."

He cupped her cheek with his hand, stroked her skin with the pad of his thumb. "I need you to trust me. This is hard. I understand that more than you know. But emotions won't find Polly. We have to operate on the facts, on logic and motive. There's no room for anything else."

Tears welled up in her eyes. She wanted to shout at him that he was wrong, but the ache in her throat held back the words.

"If no one close to Polly is involved," he said softly, "then we have to assume that the person who did this had other motives. Motives that will in all likelihood ensure a bad outcome."

A sob ripped from her throat. Melissa tried to hold it back but the agony would not be contained.

Jonathan pulled her into his arms. She'd missed having him hold her this way.

"The chances that this was a stranger are minimal. If not a family member, it's definitely someone you know. Maybe well."

Melissa closed her eyes and burrowed her face in his shirt. His scent filled her and made her want to stay in his arms until this horror had passed. *Dear God, who would do this?*

"We'll get to the truth," he promised. "But it won't be easy and no one is going to like the route we have to take to get there."

He'd said that before and on some level she understood that he was all too right. Melissa lifted her face to his. "The chief interviewed all of us. Anyone who had any contact with Polly whatsoever." Surely a man with as much law enforcement experience as the chief would have picked up on any discrepancies.

"Unfortunately, he's too close to the people in this town. Like you, he's not going to believe anyone here is capable of this sort of evil. With Floyd Harper's sudden death, the chief seems to be convinced Stevie Price is the culprit. Narrowing his suspect pool that way defeats his efforts before he even starts."

Jonathan's assessment made sense. She knew this. "I'm so tired." She leaned her cheek against his chest and tried to borrow his strength to chase away all the horrible thoughts and images in her mind.

"You rest." He caressed her hair. "I'm not going anywhere until we figure this out."

She'd wondered so many times during the past three years if he'd moved on to someone new. If he'd gotten married. But she didn't see a ring. The urge to ask him was suddenly overwhelming. She understood that need for what it was, a necessary distraction. Her mind and body were beyond exhausted. She was empty, empty and desperate to be filled with something other than the agony that swelled each time she thought of Polly.

Melissa lifted her face to his. "Will you stay here?" The look on his face told her she needed to explain. "There's plenty of room. It's just me rambling around in this old house." Heat flushed her cheeks. Could she not have worded her explanation a little differently?

"If that's what you want."

What she wanted was for him to take her to bed and help her forget the misery for just one night.

But that would be a mistake. Her heart couldn't take losing him again.

"Good." That she managed the one word without her voice shaking was a miracle. "I'll show you to William's old room."

When she would have turned away, he pulled her back to face him. "There's just one thing I need to get out of the way first," he said, his voice thick, his gaze intent on her mouth.

And then he kissed her.

Not a soft peck on the cheek or lips, but a hungry, raging, mouth to mouth kiss. Her arms went around his neck and he pulled her body against his. The feel of him had desire burning through her. He kissed her harder, deeper, and she lost herself in the incredible sensations.

When the need for air would no longer be ignored, he pulled his mouth from hers, but kept her forehead pressed to his. "I won't cross that line again," he vowed. "I just needed to get that out of the way."

"Okay." She couldn't catch her breath anymore than he could.

"I'll get my bag from the rental car."

And just like that he walked away, leaving her standing there, even hungrier and needier than before.

Melissa recognized one absolute certainty. Jonathan Foley was a man of his word. If he said he wouldn't cross that line again, he wouldn't.

Unless she dragged him over it.

# Chapter Nine

*10:00 p.m.*

Scott parked his car alongside the dirt road and sat in the dark for several minutes.

He'd followed Harry Shepherd here just before dark. The narrow deserted road made tailing him damned hard considering there was no traffic in which to blend. Old Harry obviously had had other things on his mind. Otherwise he'd surely have noticed Scott in his rearview mirror.

Scott had stayed way, way back, mind you. But even at dusk and with his headlights off, the man should have noticed a vehicle following him. All the more reason to be suspicious.

Harry was up to no good.

Now, well after dark, Scott had returned. He would soon know what Harry had been up to.

Fumbling for his flashlight, Scott wrapped the fingers of one hand around his granddaddy's shotgun and snatched up the flashlight with the other. His granddaddy had used the shotgun to keep the riffraff run off his place. When he'd died he'd left it to Scott. Scott had done a mental eye roll at the time. Like he would ever shoot a gun for any reason.

But he'd matured since then. He now knew that there was a time when a man had to do things he didn't like to do. Like carry a gun. He wasn't about to go into those woods without something to defend himself. His granddaddy's shotgun would do just fine. Luther Stubblefield at the hardware store had suggested buckshot since Scott wasn't an accomplished marksman. All he had to do was get close enough, and the buckshot would spread out in a wide pattern when fired, making it pretty difficult to miss a target.

The remark had offended Scott. So he'd opted for the kind of ammo that would take down an elephant. Besides, Scott had no fear of missing if anyone got in his face. In particular, he was not afraid of Harry Shepherd. Whatever he was hiding in that old dilapidated shack in the woods, Scott intended to have a look.

If it was that child, Polly, he also intended to see that Harry Shepherd paid for his evil, conniving ways. He and that harlot Carol Talbot.

Climbing out of his car, Scott couldn't help seeing the irony in the moment. This pathetic shack was on the old Talbot place. The farm hadn't been lived on or tended in decades. The woods had taken over the clearing where the chief's great-great grandfather had homesteaded way back when. Nobody ever came out here. Not since the chief and his wife had abandoned the place after their daughter's death. Why should they come anyway? There was nothing here. It was places like this that affirmed Scott's certainty that he did not belong in Alabama. A judgeship would make his life here more tolerable, but that wasn't likely to happen for a few years yet.

As for the missing child, Scott felt confident the chief's men had given the place a cursory search when she first went missing. No doubt that move had been anticipated and she'd been moved here after the search.

Assuming she was here at all.

Scott grinned. He had a feeling. He'd spent most of his adult life watching the folks of Bay Minette. He knew everyone of them like the back of his hand. Better maybe. He had a mental file on all the sneaky ones, the cheaters, the thieves, the ones who roughed up their wives. Not a single citizen was completely innocent or without secrets.

No. They all had their secrets.

And Scott was about to blow this one wide open.

The temperature had dropped considerably since nightfall, making it a little chilly. He didn't care. Adrenaline and anticipation kept him warm enough. He would be the hero of the town when he brought that little girl home.

Finally, perhaps, William would look at Scott the way he looked at William.

Was that so much to ask?

The old shack was dark. Scott hesitated a moment. What if he were wrong? It was possible that Harry and his harlot used this place for rendezvous when the chief was less occupied with his work. Harry might have come by to retrieve something he or she had left the last time they were here.

Didn't matter. Scott was about to find out.

The weeds were hip deep as he neared the shack. There wasn't a sound, just the nocturnal insects buzzing and humming.

He stepped up onto the rickety porch. Boards creaked and moaned beneath his weight. He roamed the beam of his flashlight over the door and the boarded up windows. Still as quiet as a tomb in there.

The second thoughts he'd experienced a few moments ago were back, a little stronger this time. He reached for the rusty old knob on the door when a creak rent the air.

Scott's heart practically stalled.

He hadn't moved, and the sound hadn't come from behind him.

The door flew open, and something rushed him, toppling him to the ground.

Scott grappled to get a proper hold on the shotgun, despite the strong hands that manacled his arms. Male. Big. Strong. Filthy smelling. The two rolled on the ground, grunting and heaving.

Finally a blast exploded in the air, nearly shattering his ear drums.

The man's weight slumped atop Scott.

He lay perfectly still, waiting, afraid to even breathe.

The man still didn't move.

Scott shoved him off. Shaking all over, he tossed the shotgun aside and scrambled to his feet. Had he fired the shotgun? He wiped his hands on his trousers.

What the hell had just happened?

He nudged the heap on the ground with his foot. The man didn't move.

Scott swallowed hard. Where was his flashlight? He felt around on the ground, working his way back toward the porch. His fingers finally wrapped around the hard plastic cylinder. He clicked it on and swept the beam over the ground until it landed on the heap.

The big man lay face down on the ground. Blood seeped from beneath him. Scott looked down at himself, turned the flashlight on his torso.

His breath caught when he saw blood.

Was he hurt?

He felt around on his chest, his abdomen. He was okay. Must be the other man's blood.

Easing closer, he tried to identify the man on the ground. He couldn't see his face. Holding his breath, Scott leaned and rolled the man over.

The squeak that echoed in the air came from Scott.

The man was Stevie Price.

Why had Stevie attacked him?

Scott stared at the gun on the ground. Because he'd sneaked up on him at night with a shotgun in his hand.

"Dear God." He'd killed a man. A mentally challenged man.

There would be no plea bargaining his way out of this. His daddy's money wouldn't buy him a get-out-of-jail-free card—

Had he heard that? A whimpering sound that brushed against his senses. His ears perked up, and this time he was certain. It was a soft, sad sound.

Scott whipped around and shone the light on the shack.

"Who's there?"

Faint cries whispered on the night air.

He moved cautiously forward, inching closer and closer to the shack.

"Hello?"

The crying didn't let up. Soft sobbing.

The porch creaked when he stepped onto it again. Scott braced for another attack that never came. He stepped gingerly through the open door. The place smelled bad, almost as bad as Stevie. Poor, stupid misfit. Scott put his hand over his mouth and shone the light around the room. In the beam of light he saw a sleeping bag. Bottled water. Food remains. And something in the corner. Something pink.

A dress.

Scott's heart almost stilled again.

In the corner, curled in a little ball, was a blond-haired child.

He swallowed back a lump of emotion. "Polly?"

Big tear-filled eyes looked up at him.

It was her. William's child.

A howl shattered the silence, and Scott whirled to face the sound. Before he could wonder where his shotgun was, something hit him in the stomach, knocking him to the floor.

The flashlight spun across the room.

Scott blinked as a fire lit in his belly. He touched himself and felt the warm, sticky wetness. He held his hand in front of his face. The meager glow from the flashlight on the other side of the room highlighted something dark on his fingers. Blood. His blood.

Agony swelled in his midsection.

He'd been shot.

Before he could cry out, the barrel of a shotgun appeared between his eyes. His gaze traced the long black barrel and settled upon the face staring down at him.

He opened his mouth and tried to speak but he couldn't seem to form the words. What was wrong with him? Finally he squeaked out one word, *"You."*

This was wrong. He had to do something.

When the shotgun disappeared from his view, he tried to turn his head but couldn't.

The room started to move... No, he was moving. His body was being dragged toward the door.

He opened his mouth again to scream but the blackness swallowed him.

*11:15 p.m.*

JOHNNY RAY BRUCE sucked on the cigarette dangling from his lips. She was late. Probably couldn't get away from her old man.

Fool.

He'd told her a long time ago that she would never belong to anyone but him. Too bad she'd been too stupid to listen. Now things were way too complicated.

Headlights appeared in the distance.

Johnny Ray threw the cigarette to the ground and stamped it out. "'Bout time."

The lights flashed on the park bench next to where he'd parked his car. They didn't have to worry about being seen in the park. Folks around here went to bed with the chickens. Rolled the damned streets up at dark.

Johnny Ray hated this town. He'd have been gone long ago if it hadn't been for her.

Presley slammed the door of her car and sauntered over to him. "Gimme a smoke."

As he removed a cigarette from the pack, Johnny

Ray let his eyes skim her body. Short shorts, halter top and bare feet. Man, it was a sin for a woman to look that good. He wanted her. Right now. Right here. But she was ticked off. She didn't have to say so. He knew her well enough to read her body language like an open book.

He flipped out his lighter and watched as she drew on the cigarette. His gut tightened. She was something, all right.

She exhaled a big puff of smoke. "We got trouble."

"Oh yeah?" He lit himself another smoke. "That soldier boy of yours finally grow a brain and figure out how to make you happy?"

She rolled her eyes and took another long drag from the cigarette. "He's suspicious about that night."

"It doesn't matter how suspicious he is," Johnny Ray shot back. "He doesn't have any evidence. My uncle said there's no evidence of anything."

Presley turned away.

"Hey, baby." He put his arm around her and pulled her close. "I know this is hard, but you gotta be strong. Falling apart now won't change anything."

She jerked away from him. "My baby is missing. You don't know how that feels."

Johnny Ray shrugged. "Maybe I don't. But I don't like it when you mope around like this."

She lifted her chin haughtily. "He says I can't talk to you anymore."

Rage roared through Johnny Ray. He charged up toe-to-toe with her. "So what? He's said that before. His threats have never changed anything."

"He says he'll get a divorce."

"Hey!" Johnny Ray threw up his arms. "That's great. He should've come up with that plan years ago."

She glared at him. "I don't want a divorce. That would leave me with no insurance. No money. Nothing. I'm not living that way again. And…"

"And what?" he snared.

"Maybe I don't want to lose him."

Another rush of fury stormed Johnny Ray. "What're you saying?"

"That I can't see you anymore." She shook with her own anger and no small measure of fear.

She was actually serious.

Johnny Ray laughed. Long and loud. She glared at him. "Well, darling, I'm afraid that doesn't work for me."

She tossed the cigarette away. "Well," she mocked him, "I guess you'll just have to deal with it."

Johnny Ray stuck his face in hers. "I don't think so. You'll do whatever I tell you to."

"I'm through letting you run me. I deserve better and Will wants me to be happy."

"Sounds like your sister-in-law's been filling your head with fairy tales again."

"Melissa's been better to me than my own momma ever was. The Shepherds are my family." She folded her arms over her chest and shook her head. "I'm not cheating on Will anymore." Her chin quivered but she held it high. "We're done, Johnny Ray."

Shaking his head, he chuckled. "Well," he said cruelly, "you should've thought of that before you killed his kid."

Behind her, tires squealed.

Johnny Ray looked past Presley to see William's truck skid to a stop next to her car. The soldier boy jumped out, leaving the door open.

"Johnny Ray," William snarled, "you're a dead man."

"Call my uncle," Johnny Ray said to Presley as he walked past her. To William he taunted, "Bring it on, soldier boy. Let's see if the military made a man out of you after all."

*Saturday, May 29th, 1:02 a.m.*

MELISSA SHOOK LOOSE from the dream. It was the same one she had whenever Jonathan was on her mind. They were still together. He hadn't left, and they had children of their own.

A howl shattered the final remnants of sleep.

Melissa sat up. A curse hissed through the air.

*Jonathan.*

She threw back the covers and jumped up. When she reached the door to William's room her brain had only just conjured up the idea that she shouldn't go to Jonathan like this. It was too late.

He sat on the side of the bed, his hands braced on either side of him.

"You okay?" she asked him.

"Yes."

That was his stock answer. She crossed the room, using the moonlight filtering in between the curtains to avoid the clothing littering the floor, and sat down beside him.

"The same old nightmares?"

He nodded.

"I don't suppose you want to talk about it." He never had. Three years apart likely hadn't changed his mind about sharing with her.

"I led my team behind enemy lines."

Shock radiated through Melissa. He was going to tell her? Now? Fear of shattering the moment kept her from speaking.

"We were captured. As soon as I was identified, the interrogation started. They knew I had information that would help their cause."

She wanted to touch him, to put her arms around him and hold him close but she didn't dare move. The pain in his voice tore at her heart.

"When I wouldn't break, they moved on to another technique."

The ability to breathe eluded her.

"They tortured and killed my men, one at a time, in an attempt to make me talk."

Dear God. How could anyone hope to recover from that kind of trauma?

"I didn't break. I couldn't let my country down."

He fell silent for so long Melissa thought he'd finished. She reached out to him, but he flinched.

"They all died for nothing. The mission was aborted after our capture. But I didn't know." He shook his head. "I didn't know."

Melissa put her arms around him. He tried to draw away but she held on tight. "I'm sorry," she whispered. "You did your duty. That's all you could do."

He pressed his cheek to hers. "They died for nothing."

The agony in his voice had tears welling in her eyes. "They died for their country," she murmured. "It was all any of you could do." Though she didn't understand exactly what had happened, she knew full well if his men had been anything like Jonathan, any one of them would have done the same thing he had.

He turned his mouth around to hers. "I swore I wouldn't do this again."

"You don't have to," she whispered, her lips brushing his. "I'll do it."

A ringing sound made her hesitate. The phone.

For a moment she couldn't move. She could only breathe the same air as him.

The phone rang again.

"I have to get that." She forced her body to draw away from his and stood, then she practically ran. All the way back to her room. She snatched the phone from the nightstand. "Hello."

"Melissa."

"What's wrong, Uncle Harry? Have they found Polly?" Fear lodged in her throat. The sweet sensual heat Jonathan had stirred vanished in a heartbeat.

The overhead light came on and Jonathan stood in her doorway.

"It's William," Harry said, his voice haunted.

Melissa looked around for her clothes. "Is he okay?"

"He and Johnny Ray had a fight. Johnny Ray's beat up pretty bad. The chief's holding William until we come pick him up."

Melissa closed her eyes and scrubbed at them. Why in God's name didn't Johnny Ray admit defeat? Presley had chosen William. "I'll be right there."

"I'm on my way to city hall to pick up William. You stay put. I'll bring him back to the house and we'll try to talk some sense into him."

"Okay. Be careful." It was the middle of the night and Harry wasn't so young anymore. Melissa hung up the phone and met Jonathan's questioning gaze. "William and Johnny Ray got into a fight. Johnny Ray's in the hospital. Uncle Harry's going to pick up William from city hall."

"Has he been charged?"

Melissa sighed. "I don't know." She combed her fingers through her hair. How could any of them do this with Polly missing? It was insane.

"Where's his wife?"

Melissa shook her head. "I didn't think to ask."

For the first time since he walked in, she noticed Jonathan was staring at her. Heat rushed into her cheeks as she realized the state of her dress.

"Sorry." She wrapped her arms around her middle, covering her breasts. The nightgown was thin and from the look in Jonathan's eyes, he saw right through the fabric.

Jonathan took a step into the room. "I've seen every inch of you, Melissa."

The heat that had infused her cheeks started anew deep in her belly. "I know, but that was before." She pulled in a much needed breath. "I didn't mean to come into your room like that." What had she been thinking? If that phone hadn't rung, God knows what would have happened.

"I'm glad you did."

Their gazes collided and held. He'd dragged on his jeans but hadn't taken the time to fasten them. He was as lean and strong as she remembered and the need to touch him, every part of him, made her knees weak. But she couldn't go there, not and survive. Losing him had been too hard. That he'd shared his nightmare with her only made being together more difficult. Bruises, maybe a few days old, were scattered on his torso. She frowned. She hadn't asked what kind of work he did now.

As if he sensed the war going on inside her and

the questions the bruises raised, he nodded. "I'll be waiting in the living room."

Melissa held her breath until he'd walked away.

By the time she'd gotten dressed and pulled herself together, Uncle Harry had arrived with William and Presley in tow. William had a black eye, a swollen lip and a few scratches. Johnny Ray on the other hand had a mild concussion and two cracked ribs.

"The chief isn't pressing charges considering," Harry explained.

"Considering what?" Jonathan asked.

William, she noticed, didn't say a word. Neither did Presley. She sat on the sofa next to her husband, her legs crossed and her foot tapping a hundred miles an hour.

Taking a breath, Melissa sat down next to Presley. "You okay?"

Presley wouldn't meet her gaze, just shook her head.

"You want me to tell them?"

Melissa looked up at her uncle who'd asked the question. Harry starred at William who sat there, unblinking.

"William?" Melissa said softly. "We can talk later, if you'd prefer." She turned to Harry. "They're both exhausted. This has been—"

"She wasn't home when Polly disappeared," William said abruptly.

Melissa's heart bumped hard against her sternum.

"She was with him."

Presley stared at the floor where her foot tapped faster and faster.

"Dear God," Harry groaned. "How could you do that to William?" Harry demanded. "He deserves better."

The silence that held the room captive for the next few seconds weighed several tons.

Presley nodded. "He made me."

"Who made you?" Jonathan prompted. Melissa greatly appreciated the sympathy in his voice.

"Johnny Ray."

William's face tightened. Melissa wished she could protect him from this.

"How so?" Jonathan nudged.

Harry stood. "I can't listen to any more of this." He gestured to the door. "I'll be on the porch."

Presley glanced at Melissa, then at Jonathan. "He blackmailed me. He said if I didn't meet him whenever he asked, he'd tell Will my secret."

Before Melissa could launch into a rant about what she'd like to do to Johnny Ray, Jonathan asked in that same gentle voice, "Can you share that secret with us now?"

Presley nodded. She stole a look at William. "After Will deployed to Afghanistan, I found out I was pregnant again." She made a keening sound and her lips trembled. "You know I couldn't handle another kid." This she said to Melissa. "I can barely take care of Polly."

"Dear God." Melissa knew where this was going.

"So I got Johnny Ray to take me to Birmingham and I had an abortion."

William lunged to his feet and walked out onto the porch with Harry.

Presley broke down, dropped her face into her hands. "I should've been home that night. But he made me meet him. I wasn't gone long. I thought Polly was in her room when I got back but I was really drunk."

Melissa wanted to hate her for what she'd done, but she couldn't. She set aside the fact that Presley had just admitted terminating a baby she had conceived with Will. Presley had been abused her whole life. She wasn't equipped to deal with snakes like Johnny Ray.

Melissa pulled the younger woman into her arms. "You should've told me. I would've made sure he never bothered you again." Will had trusted Melissa to watch over Polly and Presley. But she couldn't do that if Presley wasn't honest with her.

Presley sobbed harder. "I didn't want you to hate me. Now look what I've done."

It no longer mattered that Melissa was right— Presley had been holding something back. But her revelation changed nothing.

Polly was still missing.

# Chapter Ten

*8:30 a.m.*

Jonathan followed the chief and his deputies around the perimeter that had been cordoned off as a crime scene.

Stevie Price's body had been discovered early that morning by two teenagers. The young men had insisted they'd come to the shack for a weekend of fishing in the nearby river. Judging by what the police had found in their vehicle, fishing hadn't been on the agenda. More like partying. Lots of beer and chips, and no sign of any fishing gear.

Stevie Price had been shot in the chest once. The coroner had concluded that Price had died within seconds of being hit. An autopsy would likely show the round had ripped through his heart.

Inside the shack, considerable evidence indicated that Polly Shepherd had been held there. But there was no sign of the child now.

More frightening was the blood trail that led from the floor of the shack, across the porch and deep into the woods. The blood had run out but the evidence that a body had been dragged had not.

Chief Talbot lifted his hand. "Hold up."

Jonathan studied the ground in front of the chief. A broken clump of small tree limbs indicated that perhaps whoever had been dragged wasn't quite dead at that point.

Talbot crouched down and inspected the ragged brush. "Those forensics techs here yet?"

"Ten minutes out, Chief," one of the deputies reported.

Talbot shook his head. "We need them now."

Jonathan scanned the woods in front of them. The hum of the river was louder now. They were close. His instincts warned that the body—whoever it belonged to—had been dumped in the river. Perhaps while the victim was still alive.

Jonathan crouched down near the chief. "This trail appears to be too large for a child's body. The perp would simply have carried the child." That was the only good thing about this day so far.

He glanced back toward the shack. Melissa and her uncle were being detained at the road. They didn't need to see any of this...not until they knew something conclusive about the victim.

"I'd say you're right." The chief pushed to his feet. "Looks like we're headed to the river."

The chief's face had paled. He took out a handkerchief and dabbed at his forehead.

The two deputies trailing their steps stared at the

ground. Jonathan was clearly missing something here. As the chief moved forward, Jonathan hung back, falling into step with the deputies.

"Man, this sucks," the deputy to Jonathan's right mumbled.

"It does," Jonathan agreed.

The deputy shook his head. "More than you know."

The other deputy cleared his throat and exchanged a look with his colleague.

Jonathan slowed his step, hoping to slow the progress of the other two men. "What does that mean?" he asked when the chief was several meters ahead.

"This is the river where his daughter drowned." The one who'd spoken nodded toward the chief.

"He and his family used to come here in the summer and fish and swim," the other deputy said. He shook his head. "This place has been deserted since that little girl died."

Jonathan processed the information. Why would someone keep Polly Shepherd hidden away here of all places? The better question at the moment was who killed Stevie Price? And who else had been murdered in this place? Judging by the amount of blood the victim who'd been dragged had lost, it was unlikely he or she would've survived in or out of the water.

Why had Stevie bought a bus ticket for Nashville and then hidden away out here? From what Melissa had told him, Stevie lacked the mental capacity to formulate such a complex plan. Jonathan looked up and around at the thick canopy of trees that almost completely blocked the morning sun.

The tree line broke as the land disappeared into the murky water. Chief Talbot was moving faster now. Jonathan quickened his pace to catch up to him.

When they reached the water's edge, the chief staggered a bit. Jonathan moved up behind him, covertly steadying him. The chief glanced at him, a glimmer of gratitude amid the agony in his eyes.

The deputies scoured the shoreline. Jonathan studied the rocks protruding in the shallower sections of the water. "There." He pointed to a cluster of rocks down river. Barely visible was something light green or bluish.

Chief Talbot waded into the water.

"Chief, wait," one of the deputies called after him. "I can do that."

The chief kept going, trudging through the hip deep water toward what appeared to be a body trapped between two large boulders.

Jonathan was right behind him. He consoled himself with the fact that the body—if it was a body—was far too large to be Polly's.

The chief stumbled. Jonathan helped him up then plunged forward to reach what was indeed a body, face down, caught between the rocks. He touched the carotid artery. Definitely dead.

"This one didn't make it, either," Jonathan said as the chief approached.

Talbot steadied himself and nodded to the body. "Turn it over," he said to his deputies. "Let's see who this is and get 'em out of this damned river."

The two deputies wrestled the bloated body free of the rocks and turned the man face up.

Scott Rayburn.

"Holy Moses," the chief muttered.

"We'll get him to the bank," one of the deputies said. He looked almost as pale as the chief.

Talbot motioned for the two to get on with it. He plowed through the water, stopped midway to the bank and surveyed the area.

Jonathan stayed close by. The man had the look of one about to keel over.

"This just doesn't make sense," the chief said more to himself than to Jonathan. "Why would Stevie and Rayburn do something like this?"

Jonathan didn't have to point out the obvious. A third party was involved. He understood what the chief meant. Why would either man be involved in abducting Polly Shepherd?

"I guess this explains why Harper is dead."

Chief Talbot shot Jonathan a look. "I'd say so."

Harper had lied, it would seem, about seeing Price get on the bus. Whoever had prompted him to do so had obviously gotten nervous and tied up that loose end. But why? What did Harper and Price have in common? And what did that have to do with Rayburn's accusations against Harry Shepherd, if anything? Was there bad blood between the elder Shepherd and Rayburn?

Not according to Melissa.

"Oh, Lord, have mercy."

The chief fell against Jonathan. "I've got you." As soon as the man was steadied, he lunged through the water. "Wait, Chief…"

Then Jonathan saw what had captured the chief's attention, what had taken him to his knees.

Amid the thick growth lining the shore a dozen or so meters away a small blond head bobbed in the water.

Jonathan bounded forward, the water pulling at his legs. His heart rocketed into his throat.

*No. No. No. Don't let it end like this.*

He reached the bushes before the chief. Jonathan reached through the limbs and closed his fingers around the…doll.

Jonathan's knees gave out under him. He sank into the water, its murkiness lapping at his neck. The chief practically fell on top of him.

"Let me see. For God's sake, let me see."

Jonathan held the doll up for his inspection.

A sob tore from the chief's throat.

It was a while before either of them could walk back to shore. By the time they reached Rayburn's body and the two deputies, the forensics techs had arrived.

Chief Talbot sat down on the ground and held his head in his hands.

The deputies worked with the techs to attempt recovering any trace evidence. At some point the coroner arrived to examine the body.

Jonathan watched, unable to speak or act. When he'd seen the blond head in the water all he'd been able to think about, besides the tragic loss of a child, was what this would do to Melissa, and to her family.

He closed his eyes and blocked the kind of pain he hadn't allowed in in years. Not since he'd watched his men, his squad, die one by one because he refused to talk. To sell out his country.

That was when he'd stopped allowing himself to feel. Melissa had stirred the desire to feel again, but he'd blocked her out, too.

He'd stopped being human and he'd lost her because of it.

Jonathan opened his eyes. Fury tightened his jaw. Whoever had done this to her and her family, he would find them and he would make them pay.

Chief Talbot managed to pull himself together enough to finish the job he'd come here to do. He gave the order to drag the river.

If the doll was confirmed as belonging to Polly, and Jonathan felt certain it would be, the next step would be to search for her body.

He needed to break this news to Melissa before she heard it from the crowd that had in all inevitability gathered at the road. The news vultures would be monitoring the police band.

MELISSA WAS LOSING her mind.

Why didn't one of the deputies come back and tell them something? They'd been gone nearly an hour. She scanned the crowd that had gathered. Dozens of Bay Minette citizens stood alongside media crews, waiting for news.

William had been restrained when he'd attempted to breach the crime scene. Presley sat in the back seat of the patrol car with him. Both were out of their minds with grief and guilt.

A rumble in the crowd drew her attention back to the woods in time to see Jonathan appear. Melissa's heart thundered. Fear closed around her throat as he came near enough for her to see his grim face.

His clothes were wet.

Her knees began to buckle but she locked them, held on to her uncle's arm.

Jonathan crossed under the yellow tape and was immediately assaulted by reporters. He pushed through without a word. His right arm went around Melissa. "Let's get out of here."

"What happened?" Harry demanded.

"Not here," Jonathan warned.

Melissa's head spun. She and Harry clung to each other as Jonathan said something to the deputy at the car where Will and Presley waited. Then he ushered Melissa and her uncle to her car.

The reporters tried again to get some answers or at least a comment. Jonathan's lethal glare shut them up in an instant.

"What happened back there?" Melissa demanded when they were driving away from the persistent reporters. "Was it really Stevie?"

Jonathan put a hand over hers. "We'll talk when we get to your house."

When Melissa would have argued, he added, "We didn't find Polly."

Melissa wasn't sure whether to be relieved or more worried. For now, she chose the former. At least there was still hope that Polly was alive. When the call had come about Stevie… She closed her eyes. How could this be? Stevie had been like a part of her family.

The twenty minutes it took to reach her house felt like a lifetime. The utter silence had been deafening and agonizing. She'd wanted to ask so many other questions but she'd been afraid of the answers. Harry had sat in the backseat, apparently suffering the same horrific fear.

Will and Presley arrived right behind them. When they were all inside, seated, braced for the worst, Jonathan finally broke his silence.

"Stevie was shot," he explained. "We're not sure by whom, but…"

Melissa couldn't imagine who would want to shoot Stevie. Maybe he'd discovered where Polly was being held and the person who'd taken her had shot him.

"Scott Rayburn's body was found, too. He'd been shot, as well."

"What?" Will demanded. "That's crazy."

Presley broke down into sobs.

Harry simply sat there. He said nothing and looked at no one. Melissa worried about him. He wasn't a young man anymore. As hard as this was on her, it was worse for him, on a physical level.

Jonathan shook his head. "There are no answers yet." He sat down on the sofa arm next to Melissa. "There was evidence that a child was being held in the shack."

"What kind of evidence?" Will was on his feet now instead of comforting his wife. "They should've let me in there."

"Toys. A couple of changes of clothes—girl's clothing."

Jonathan kept his voice steady and calm but his words ripped Melissa's insides to shreds. "Was there anything else?" Please don't let him say blood.

"There was some blood inside," he explained, "but the preliminary estimation is that it belongs to Rayburn. It appears he was shot in the shack and then dragged to the river."

The idea that the chief's child had drowned in that river hit Melissa hard. What the man must have gone through. "But Polly wasn't there?" Melissa looked up at Jonathan. "This doesn't make sense. Two people are dead." She shook her head. "Three counting Floyd Harper. And Polly is still missing."

Jonathan scrubbed a hand over his face.

There was more. Melissa's heart sank. "What?" she demanded. It might have been three years, but she knew that look. "What aren't you telling us?"

"When we found Rayburn's body…" He struggled to find the right words, the battle playing out on his face. "In the water, there was a doll, too."

Presley sat up straight. "Pink dress?" she demanded. "Blond hair?" Her voice grew higher and tighter with every word.

Jonathan hesitated then said, "Yes."

Presley cried out in anguish. William collapsed onto the sofa next to her.

Melissa felt numb. She couldn't cry. She couldn't ask any more questions.

Jonathan exhaled a troubled breath. "The chief has ordered a team to drag the river."

Surely that river hadn't taken another child, Melissa thought. God wouldn't be that cruel.

"I have to go…" Harry stood. He looked around as if he were lost. "I need to help."

Melissa pushed to her feet, wobbled a little. "There's nothing you can do right now, Uncle Harry."

He shook his head. "I have to go."

Before Melissa could say more he rushed out the door.

Melissa looked from Jonathan to her brother and his wife.

They were all a mess. There was nothing they could do for Polly.

They had failed.

*Pull yourself together.* The inner voice reminded her of her resolve to be strong. She dragged in a broken breath. "I'm calling Dr. Ledford. He can call in something for Presley." Presley cried hysterically. The sound was devastating.

At the mention of his wife's name, Will met Melissa's gaze. "It would be better if Presley got some rest now," she told him. "Maybe you, too."

He shook his head. "I need to be out there." His voice was hollow, weak.

Melissa didn't argue with him. He was right. His daughter was missing. He needed to be out there. She nodded. "You go. I'll take care of Presley." Melissa walked to the window and checked the drive. "Uncle Harry's still out there. Ride with him," she said to William.

She worried about Harry. He'd rushed out of the house then just sat there in the car. He would need William with him. They needed each other.

When her brother had gone, Melissa made the call. Dr. Ledford's nurse, a friend of hers, promised to call the drugstore immediately and have someone deliver a sedative for Presley.

Melissa tucked Presley into the bed William had slept in growing up, then she wandered back into the living room. Jonathan was on the phone.

She stared out the kitchen window at the swing Polly loved to play on whenever she stayed over. Melissa could imagine the little girl swinging high, her blond hair flying behind her. She was the sweetest child.

Melissa refused to believe she was dead.

She was out there, waiting to be found.

And then everything would be all right. Just like her Uncle Harry said.

It had to be.

Jonathan ended his call and joined her at the window. "You need to eat."

Melissa shook her head. There was no way she could eat right now.

"There's not much else we can do until we hear from the chief," Jonathan offered. "I'll fix you one of my famous omelets and we'll review what we know so far. See what we can figure out."

What they knew was a lot of confusing details and not much else. But he was right. She needed to be strong. Part of being strong meant taking care of her basic needs. "Okay." Her lips lifted in a small smile that surprised her. "I remember your omelets. They were pretty darned awesome."

"Sit." He guided her to the table. "While I cook I want you to tell me more about Stevie Price and Polly."

Melissa felt sick to her stomach. Why would Stevie do this?

Jonathan pilfered through cabinets and the fridge until he'd gathered everything he needed. He prodded Melissa for answers as he worked.

She did the best she could, but that old, ugly fear kept vying for her attention.

Polly's doll had been in the river with Scott Rayburn's body. Images of Polly's favorite doll floating in that murky river kept flashing in Melissa's brain.

The hope Melissa had been holding on to slipped from her grasp...

# Chapter Eleven

*12:03 p.m.*

"I did this."

Harry sat in his car, staring straight ahead at nothing.

Polly was gone.

Stevie was dead.

What in the world had Rayburn done? How had he found Stevie and Polly?

If they found that baby in the water... Harry's fingers squeezed into fists. There would be only one thing he could do.

He'd left William with the search team, but Harry had needed to talk to her. She was the only one who would understand.

"No," Carol argued. "You didn't do this. Something went wrong." She curled her arms around him, tried to comfort him. "It wasn't supposed to be like this."

Harry couldn't look at her. If he did, she would see the ugly truth in his eyes. He was a monster. One who had caused the death of his precious Polly. One who had destroyed his nephew. William would never forgive him. As well he shouldn't.

"Rayburn did this," Carol insisted. "He spent every waking moment attempting to stir trouble. To hurt someone." She pressed her forehead to Harry's arm. "Now he's done it. He's ruined everything."

"I was there," Harry said, his voice coming from a hollow place inside him. "Before dark last night. Stevie and Polly were fine. She…" He swallowed back the lump in his throat. "She was playing with that doll."

"Who else could have known?" Carol asked softly, the plea nearly more than he could bear.

Harry had no answer. No one had known. Only the two of them. Stevie hadn't understood. He'd thought he was babysitting for a few days. Floyd Harper hadn't known. He'd just done what Harry paid him to do. Until he'd decided he needed more money.

Dear God, Harry hadn't meant to kill him. It had been an accident. The old fool had tried to force Harry to give him more money—for an operation he'd claimed he needed. But that wasn't true. He'd have spent on liquor whatever Harry had given him. They'd argued and the crazy man had charged Harry. What else could he have done? He'd pushed the man off him. He hadn't realized they were standing so close to the edge of that bridge.

Now he was dead. And Stevie, as well.

Agony swelled inside Harry. Sweet, innocent little Polly was likely dead, too.

Dear God, this was all his doing.

He was a monster who didn't deserve to live.

"It's best that we don't see each other again." His empty words echoed in the confined space.

Carol stared at him. He didn't have to look at her to know. He could feel her gaze upon him. She was as devastated as he was. Except none of this was her fault.

"You can't mean that," she whispered.

"You'll only be hurt when the truth comes out." He closed his eyes to block the painful image of that doll floating in the water. The doll kept morphing into Polly. Lord, just strike him dead now.

"I don't care." She held more tightly on to him. "Reed will retire and move to Gatlinburg. I'll stay here with you. We'll get through this together."

Harry shook his head. "There won't be any getting through it." He turned to her. "Go with Reed, Carol. He's a good man. You deserve better than me."

Tears welled in her eyes. "You promised we would be together. Finally. After all this time."

"No one will ever know about us." He turned his attention back to the road. "That's the way it has to be. It's the only way to protect you. I've hurt too many people already."

"I won't let you do this," she cried. "I know what you're thinking."

She couldn't. She wasn't a monster like him. She couldn't possibly know.

"You believe everyone will be better off without you." She shook him. "That's wrong, Harry. You'll just hurt them all the more. You did what you thought was right—what would save Will. You had no idea this would happen. Rayburn messed everything up."

"No." Harry let go a weary breath. "I messed everything up. This is my doing."

"Will and Melissa will forgive you in time," she urged.

"They won't." They shouldn't. He didn't deserve forgiveness.

"Then they don't have to know." She reached up and caressed his jaw. "Why should any of them ever know? There is no evidence linking you to what happened. No one ever has to know."

If only it were that easy. "I'll know." And he couldn't live with it.

"I won't let you do this, Harry."

He patted her hand. Carol meant well, but she didn't understand. He had hurt the people he loved most. He had caused that sweet baby's death.

There was only one thing to do now.

Even if by some miracle Polly was found unharmed, he had caused three deaths. No matter who pulled the trigger, he was responsible.

He had to pay.

# Chapter Twelve

*4:30 p.m.*

The team dragging the river had found nothing so far.

William had just delivered the news, but he still refused to leave the scene. Harry, he told her, had left hours ago, but every time she called, he didn't answer his cell phone. Melissa was really worried about him. She wanted to go and find him, but William made her promise to stay with Presley. Finally giving in to the effects of the medication, she was sleeping soundly.

Jonathan had been back and forth. He called or came home every hour or so to check on her. He was the single reason she felt comfortable staying behind. She knew that Jonathan would do whatever needed to be done.

Melissa peeked in on Presley again. She was out. Most folks couldn't understand the patience and sympathy Melissa felt for Presley. They didn't comprehend how hard her life had been. Other than the

Johnny Ray thing, Presley had come a long way. She tried hard. Some people just weren't strong enough to stand up to someone like Johnny Ray. Presley had been used and abused by him. Her childhood had deeply instilled in her that she didn't deserve any better. She'd once told Melissa that she didn't know why Will loved her. Johnny Ray had exploited that doubt.

Whatever pain he suffered as a result of the beating he'd taken from William, the bastard deserved.

Melissa picked up the phone and tried both Harry's cell and his house phone. Still no answer.

"Dammit." Where was he?

A soft rap at the front door snapped her from the troubling thought. Fear fired through her. Wouldn't Jonathan have called if there was news?

Not if it was bad.

Fear sucking at her composure, she trudged to the front door. She checked past the curtain.

Her heart battered her chest wall as she saw Jonathan. She opened the door. Her gaze collided with his and she wanted to ask—to demand—what he'd learned, but terror held her tongue.

"They're still searching," he explained, "but they haven't found her. That could be a good sign."

Relief made Melissa sway. "Thank God."

"The team leader said that with the lack of strength behind the current, even a small body wouldn't have been carried far. They're cautiously optimistic that she isn't in the water."

Melissa fell against him. She couldn't help herself. She needed his strong arms around her. And she cried. Her niece was still missing but at least she wasn't in that damned river.

Jonathan led her back into the living room after he closed the door. "The thinking now is that she may have run. The chief's broadening the search grid in hopes of finding some trace of her in the woods."

"Then there's still hope." The weather wasn't a real issue. She'd been well fed, based on the evidence found at the shack, and clothed. There was reason to hold out hope. But searching the acres and acres of those woods could take too long.

"There's hope." He caressed her cheek and offered a smile. "The thrust of the investigation now is determining how Price and Rayburn were connected. There has to be a motive for their actions. If we learn the motive, we'll be far more likely to find her."

Melissa gave herself a shake. Jonathan looked exhausted. She hadn't considered that he'd scarcely had any sleep, either, much less anything to eat. "Would you like coffee? Or tea?" She really knew better than to ask about the tea. Jonathan didn't go for the Southern tradition of iced tea.

He shook his head. "I'm fine."

"Are you sure?" She searched his face, her pulse skipping at the memories of all they had shared. So many nights she had lain beside him and watched him sleep. She'd loved him so much…still did. But she would never admit that out loud.

"I need to talk to you about Rayburn and the accusations he made when he approached me."

The memory infuriated her all over again. "I hate to speak ill of the dead, but Scott Rayburn loved spreading rumors. Rumors," she reiterated. "That's what his accusations were about. I know my uncle Harry. He would never do anything like that." She blocked the memory of the perfume she'd smelled on his shirt. That didn't prove anything.

Jonathan guided her to the sofa. "Think about your uncle's reaction last night and this morning."

Now Jonathan was making her angry. "Last night he was exhausted and worried about William. This morning he was in a state of shock. We all were."

"Last night when Presley announced what she'd done," Jonathan recapped, "Harry said nothing about her leaving Polly alone. His anger was directed at the idea that she'd cheated on her husband."

"Jonathan." Melissa didn't know how to make him understand this. "All of us have already gone through a range of emotions that would put lesser folks down. Harry has been strong through all of it. But even the strongest breaks at some point. The idea that Presley was unfaithful was far less painful to latch on to." She'd witnessed it often enough as a nurse. She supposed Jonathan couldn't understand that because he was one of those rare people who had no breaking point. If she'd doubted that fact, what he'd shared with her last night about his military history confirmed her conclusion.

"Maybe so," Jonathan allowed. "I'm not so sure."

"Scott always liked being the center of attention," she said again.

"You trust your uncle that much?"

"I trust him with my life."

Jonathan's gaze held hers. "There was a time when you trusted me that much."

She had to look away. If he saw the feelings that still simmered inside her... She couldn't let that happen. Last night she'd drifted far too close to breaking down. She couldn't risk doing it again. Unlike him, she did have a breaking point.

"I need you to trust me now," he murmured. "I'm not trying to hurt you or Harry. I'm only trying to find the truth."

His soft words kicked her defenses right out from under her. "I do trust you, Jonathan." She met his searching gaze, pushed aside all the frustration. "I wouldn't have called you otherwise."

He didn't respond, just stared at her eyes, and her lips.

She wished he would say something, anything, to break the tension building between them. But he didn't. Instead, he leaned forward and brushed his lips across hers.

Melissa warned herself not to cross that line—the very one he had drawn himself. But she just couldn't help it. She was so tired. So afraid. So desperate to feel his touch. No man had ever owned her heart, but him. No man had ever made her want to grow old with him, but him. No matter that he'd left her once already, broken her heart into a million pieces, she wanted his touch. Wanted his lips against hers—just like this—as long as it would last.

So much for standing firm. She was a lost cause when it came to this man.

He kissed her slowly, softly. Just a meshing of lips. A dance of wills to see who would give in first and open in invitation.

Melissa couldn't help herself. She parted her lips, invited him inside. His tongue slid over her lips, touched her own. Her hands glided up his chest and into his hair. She loved the feel of his thick hair. Soft and silky. Such a contrast to his hard, lean body.

He drew her to her feet, without breaking the contact of their mouths. Then he scooped her into his arms and carried her into the hall.

"The last door on the right," she murmured between kisses. She didn't know why she bothered; after all, he'd spent last night here. She wasn't thinking, only feeling.

This was going to a place it shouldn't, one that would bring immense pain. But, right now, she wanted to go to that forbidden place. As much as it would hurt when he left her again, this moment— his touch—would be worth the pain of losing him a second time.

Their lives were worlds apart, their desires for the future in completely different universes. But when they made love, that all vanished. There was only her and him, coming together in such a beautiful way that she couldn't possibly resist.

Taking his time, he unbuttoned her blouse, slid it over her shoulders and down her arms. She shivered when he reached for the waistband of her jeans, which landed on the floor next to her blouse in no time. He urged her hands to do the same to him.

Button after button, she opened his shirt. When her palms slid over his smooth, warm skin, she shivered in anticipation. Her fingers fumbled with the closure of his jeans. He tried to help, but she pushed his hands away. She could do this.

She pushed his jeans and boxers down his thighs. He fumbled with shoes, finally got them off, then tugged the jeans and boxers free of his muscled legs.

As unladylike as it was, she couldn't help staring at his body. She'd loved all that muscled terrain. Every single scar was dear to her. His time in the military had taken a physical and mental toll on him. But he'd survived. No man she'd ever met was as strong as Jonathan. Not nearly.

He lifted her into his arms and settled her on the bed. She gasped when he dragged her panties down her legs and off. He cuddled in close to her, allowing her to feel the desperation in his body. He wanted this just as much as she did.

As a nurse, she understood firsthand the importance of protection. But this was Jonathan. She didn't want anything between them. He was far too responsible to risk himself or anyone else to unprotected sex if there was any danger.

She trusted him. She'd never trusted anyone the way she trusted him. With her body, her heart...her soul.

He kissed his way down her body, pleasuring her breasts with his lips and teeth. She gasped again and again. It had been so long. Three years. She hadn't been with anyone else since they first met. He'd ruined her for anyone else.

His fingers traced her hips, slid between her thighs until they found that hot, damp place that throbbed with need for him and him alone.

As much as she wanted to revel in every sensation he elicited, she wanted him to feel those same wondrous sensations. She touched him everywhere. Kissed the scar on his forehead that had first brought them together. Then his broad, muscled shoulders. That strikingly taut abdomen. His tight buttocks. Lastly she wrapped her fingers around his large sex. She shivered, felt herself moving toward release before he'd even entered her.

It had been too long.

He nestled between her thighs, nudged his way inside, one thick inch at a time. She wrapped her legs around his, dug her fingers into his hot, smooth skin. By the time he'd filled her completely, she was too far gone to slow the spiraling sensations. Climax swirled and quaked through her. Before she'd caught her breath, he found a new way to take her back to that glittering edge of release.

His mouth, his fingers…all of him played her like a concert violinist touching those precious strings. He brought her to climax again and then again before succumbing to his own.

For long, long minutes after that, he lay beside her, holding her in his powerful arms.

He kissed her cheek, her earlobe. "You are so beautiful."

She blushed. "Not so much."

He smiled, his lips stretching against her skin, making her smile, too. "You should look in a mirror occasionally. I mean really look. You're very beautiful."

"And you're very handsome." It was true. More true than she'd wanted to admit these past three years. It had been easier to deny he'd been the man of her dreams than to own out loud the suffering she'd endured with the loss of him.

"We were good together."

The words vibrated against her ear, making her heart ache. "We were."

"I don't want to hurt you again."

She turned to him, studied those gorgeous eyes. An epiphany had dawned during their lovemaking. "You can't hurt me that way again, Jonathan. That's a once in a lifetime sort of pain. It'll be hard when you go this time, but it won't ever hurt like that again." Never.

The revelation appeared to startle him, but he didn't draw away. He held her close as if he feared she would take off and he might never see her again.

He tucked a wisp of hair behind her ear. "I couldn't be what you needed me to be. What you deserved," he explained. "I still can't. You deserve better than me. As much as I want you, it wouldn't be fair to you."

She laughed softly. "That's a cop-out, you know that, right?" Men always said that crap when they had commitment issues.

He smiled. "I guess it is." He nuzzled her neck with his nose. "You were as close as I've ever come to that place." He drew back, toyed with her hair. "As much as I hurt you by leaving, it would have been far worse for me to stay. I couldn't bear seeing you suffer."

She searched his face even as she looked for the truth in his words. "Do you still have the nightmares often?"

"Too often," he confessed.

She had nightmares, too, only they were about coming home from work to find him gone.

"I should be stronger," she admitted as long as they were confessing. "Giving in to *this* wasn't such a smart thing to do in the long run." Regret, she realized, had barged in, stealing the beauty of what they had just shared.

"You didn't exactly drag me into your bed," he reminded her. "I seem to recall carrying you into the room."

Melissa laughed. For the first time in nearly a week, she just wanted to laugh. It felt good, chased away the agony for a few moments. "What do you do now?" She skimmed her fingers over his bruised abdomen. "Seems like a tough job."

"It can be." He left a trail of kisses down her belly. She shivered. "Investigative work. Nothing interesting." Before she could ask any more questions he had her ready to climax yet again. She sank into the pleasure, drew him to that hot, fiery place right along with her. This time he couldn't hold out so long—maybe because he'd missed her just as much as she'd missed him.

But he would never say as much.

He was far too secretive. Far too unbreakable.

She lured him to the shower for a few minutes more of mindless pleasure. This escape was only temporary, she knew, but she needed it so badly.

Afterwards, they dried their bodies and kissed some more. Then they ate. She hadn't been hungry in days. But she was definitely hungry now. She'd barely touched the omelet he'd gone to the trouble of preparing earlier. Anything sounded good at the moment. Cheese and crackers and the chocolate cake a neighbor had brought over. In times of crisis, Southern neighbors always brought over food. It was tradition.

For a little while, Melissa enjoyed a reprieve from the misery that had overtaken all their lives just six days ago.

There was no one else she would rather have enjoyed that time with. But as the heat of their passion receded, the glare of reality filtered in.

He would leave.

She would be hurt again. And this time there'd be no one to blame but herself.

The telephone rang. Melissa went to answer it, but someone banged on the door before she reached the phone. Confusion lining her brow, she moved to the door and checked the window.

Chief Talbot.

That old, ugly fear whipped through her, making her shake as she opened the door. "Chief." She wanted to ask if there was news, but the words wouldn't form on her tongue.

The news was bad. His face told the tale before he had an opportunity to say the words.

"Has there been a new development?" Jonathan asked, moving up beside her at the door.

The chief braced a hand against the door frame as if the news he had to pass was too heavy a burden to manage without support.

"It's Harry," he said, his voice uncharacteristically faint. "He's in the hospital."

A new kind of fear ignited inside Melissa. "Heart attack?" She'd worried about that. She'd known he was having trouble handling the building tension and worry. Dear God, she should have seen this coming and done something.

Chief Talbot shook his head. "I'm sorry, Melissa,

but he…" A weary sigh escaped his lips "He apparently attempted to kill himself."

"What?" Not Harry. He would never do that. "That can't be right," she argued.

"I'm afraid so. He left a note saying he was sorry."

Her uncle had tried to commit suicide? He'd left a note? That was impossible. He wouldn't leave them this way.

"William is at the hospital with him now." The chief shook his head. "He's in grave condition, Melissa. The prognosis isn't good."

She didn't remember getting into the car. The next thing she knew she and Jonathan were on the way to the hospital. A neighbor had come to stay with Presley and to field any calls to the house.

Melissa closed her eyes. She couldn't take any more. The idea of losing Polly was horrendous enough, but not Harry, too.

This couldn't possibly get any worse.

# Chapter Thirteen

*Sunday, May 30th, 8:01 a.m.*

Jonathan stood in the corridor of the Intensive Care Unit. Melissa had been allowed in Harry Shepherd's cubicle for ten minutes every three hours.

They'd been up all night.

Melissa refused to leave the hospital. William had rejoined the search for his daughter at daybreak this morning. Presley, his wife, was in the care of friends of the Shepherd family.

At this point, no one was considered safe from whatever was going on. Three men had been murdered, assuming Harper's death hadn't been an accident, and Harry Shepherd appeared to have attempted suicide.

Since the forensics wasn't back yet and despite the two word note he'd left, an official conclusion could not be reached. There was a chance someone had wanted his death to look like a suicide.

No matter that Jonathan's instincts leaned toward the idea that the man had wanted to take his own life, he wasn't taking any chances. He would not allow Melissa out of his sight. Leaving the hospital without her was out of the question.

The team dragging the river had called off the search at dark last night, but had resumed this morning for a final go over. Polly had not been found. Jonathan felt a massive sense of relief at that news. Melissa's family had just about reached their limit on bad news.

He closed his eyes and let the memory of last evening's lovemaking whisper through his mind. Most of his adult life had been spent focused on his career. Women came and went with the job and the location. No one had ever managed to keep a hunk of his heart.

The idea rattled him hard. He didn't try to push it away. It was the truth and that was the one ideal he'd always clung to. Truth, honor, courage, those words meant a great deal to him. Honestly, three years ago Melissa hadn't needed a man like him, nor did she now. Emotionally, he was a mess.

The military had done that for him. Not the military, really, but the powers that be. The ones who had made the final decisions, based more on political gain than on the greater good. All the while he'd watched his men die, the powers that be were finagling a new deal—one which negated the operation for which those men had given their lives.

Jonathan had sworn that he would never commit on an emotional level to anyone besides himself after that. He did his job, completed his assignments and went home—wherever home proved to be. There would be no attachments.

Then he'd met Melissa.

Bit by tiny bit, she'd taken a part of him. She'd given of herself completely, unconditionally and un-restrained. And he hadn't been able to cut it. He'd left her hanging by her heart.

He didn't deserve her forgiveness and he damned sure hadn't deserved her trust the way she'd given it last night. Hurting her again was the last thing he wanted to do. Maybe, just maybe, if he helped bring her niece back home safely, he would have earned all that Melissa had given him.

Finding Polly alive might just be impossible. But he had to try. For the child and for Melissa.

As if his thoughts had summoned her, Melissa appeared in the corridor. She looked tired and desperate for relief. Still she was so beautiful, Jonathan's chest ached. He'd never known anyone as beautiful, inside and out, as she was.

"How is he?" Only immediate family was allowed to see the patient or to be informed of his progress.

"He's still in a coma." Melissa brushed a wisp of hair from her cheek with the back of her hand. "The chances of him surviving without massive brain damage are…" her voice broke "…practically nonexistent."

Jonathan didn't hesitate. He pulled her into his

arms and held her tight. "I wish there was something I could do."

She held on to him, making him ache all the more for his helplessness. "I don't understand why he did this." She drew back and shook her head. "He's not the sort of man to do such a thing. I know he's devastated by Polly's disappearance, but we all are."

She swiped at her damp cheeks. "I can't even begin to accurately gauge how William must feel. And Presley." She shrugged. "Uncle Harry has always been a rock. I don't understand."

Jonathan needed to get her out of here for a while. She was exhausted, but there were people he wanted to see, questions he needed to ask. "You need a break."

She looked back toward her uncle's room. "I don't know about leaving."

"They have your number, right?" He slowly ushered her toward the elevator.

A hesitant nod was her only response.

"They'll call if there's any change." Since there was little chance of Harry waking up, her vigil here wouldn't help him. But there were things they could be doing to help find Polly.

"I suppose you're right."

"Your uncle would want us working on finding Polly." Jonathan didn't know the man very well but he felt certain that was the case. "I've been thinking about a couple of scenarios the chief may have overlooked."

The elevator doors slid open and they stepped inside, thankfully alone.

"You have?"

She looked at him with such desperation, it clawed at his chest. He nodded, not sure of his own voice just now.

"Anything we can do is better than nothing," she murmured wearily.

Jonathan hated the idea of dragging her around to interview the new list of persons of interest he'd developed. But he wasn't about to leave her side. Not again. He'd taken that risk yesterday, but no more.

"Where are we going first?" she asked as the elevator lit on the lobby level.

"To see Johnny Ray Bruce." After the way he had blackmailed Presley, Bruce was capable of most anything.

Surprise flared in Melissa's eyes. "Isn't he still here, in the hospital?"

Jonathan shook his head. "He was released last night."

She appeared to mull over the idea as they made their way to her car. When he opened the passenger door she hesitated before climbing inside. "Why are we talking to Johnny Ray?"

"Good question." He gestured for her to get in. When she did, he closed her door and moved around to the driver's side. After settling behind the wheel and starting the engine, he explained, "Johnny Ray was with Presley that night. He must have picked her up and taken her home since her car remained at the house all night. That's why the chief bought her story about not leaving home the night Polly disappeared." One of Presley's neighbors had confirmed that Presley's vehicle was home that night.

"True." Melissa snapped her seat belt into place.

"Johnny Ray may have seen something that felt irrelevant at the time but could be far more significant than he realizes."

In actuality, Jonathan intended to push him for information. He had known the Shepherd family his whole life. Maybe if something was going on between Harry and the chief's wife, he would have heard about it. The guy struck Jonathan as the type to keep himself in the know about secrets—especially those people desperately wanted to hide. Considering the chief was his uncle, that knowledge could have proven particularly beneficial.

"I hadn't thought about that," Melissa confessed. "I'm sure the chief didn't question him since he was unaware that Presley left the house."

"We have a bit of an advantage," Jonathan acknowledged. Presley's coming clean may have given them the break they needed. His next stop after Johnny Ray's place was Scott Rayburn's office. "Did Rayburn have a secretary?"

"He did. Frances O'Linger."

"Good. We'll need to speak to her, as well."

Melissa turned to him. "You think she may know something?"

It was a stretch, but it was definitely possible. "She may not know anything specific but she may have overheard a conversation or read a note." Jonathan pulled out onto the deserted street. "Who knows, maybe Rayburn left a journal or notes on his delusions. We won't know for sure unless we ask."

Melissa nodded. "Good points."

THE DRIVE TO JOHNNY RAY'S residence took less than ten minutes. His car sat in the driveway. If Jonathan was lucky the guy would be in a pain medication fog and considerably more cooperative.

A couple of knocks were required to get Johnny Ray to open the door. He looked every bit as woozy as Jonathan had hoped. His face showed the evidence of a serious butt-kicking.

Johnny Ray swayed forward and scanned the yard. He blinked, tried several times to focus on Melissa. "That brother of yours isn't with you, is he?"

"No," Melissa said with absolutely no sympathy. "He's out searching for his missing daughter."

"Oh." Johnny Ray swayed back on his heels.

"We need to speak with you in private," Jonathan informed him.

The man's eyebrows hiked up his forehead. "I don't know if I want you in my house." He shook his head, staggered back a step for his trouble. "Those Shepherds are nothing but trouble for me. My uncle has already threatened to haul me in if there's any more trouble."

Jonathan resisted the urge to tell him that he should have thought about that before he slept with another man's wife, repeatedly. "We'll only take a few minutes of your time. Your uncle isn't going to find out."

"Whatever." Johnny Ray turned around, braced against the wall for support and made his way to the nearest chair. "Have a seat."

His place was trashed. Not that it had been that organized or clean before, but this morning it appeared as if the man had had a party last night and the whole town had dropped off their dinner and drink remains in his living room.

"What do you wanna talk about?" he asked when both Melissa and Jonathan were seated. "As if I didn't know," he added with a drunken eye roll.

"The night Polly went missing," Jonathan began, "you picked Presley up at the house, then dropped her off. Is that correct?"

Johnny Ray bobbed his head up and down. "Will wasn't home so she came right out the front door and went back in the same way." He picked up a pack of cigarettes, dropped it, then picked it up again.

"Approximately how long was she away from the house?" Jonathan felt Melissa fidgeting next to him. He hated for her to hear this, but he didn't want her out of his sight for any reason.

"An hour I guess. Maybe less." Johnny Ray lit the cigarette and blew out a plume of smoke. He leaned forward and picked up a beer and chugged a long swallow. "We spent most of that time fighting."

"About what?" Jonathan waited patiently for him to set the can of beer back on the table and make eye contact. "About what?" he repeated.

"The fact that she refused to tell Will the truth." He shifted his attention to Melissa. "She's been lying to him for years. I keep telling her to just do the right thing and end their farce of a marriage."

Fury tightened Melissa's features. "You would know all about doing the right thing."

Johnny Ray stared at her, blinked, then turned to Jonathan. "You see. Even if I try to do the right thing I don't get any respect."

Jonathan wasn't going down that path. He'd come here to get answers not to tick him off and walk away with nothing. "Why doesn't Presley want to do this thing you believe is right?" he asked. "Maybe she loves her husband."

"Yeah, right." Johnny Ray snorted. "That would be why she likes doing it—if you know what I mean—with me more than she does him. She says there's no passion between them," he sneered.

That Melissa didn't throw something at the guy was a miracle. "So," Jonathan ventured, "the two of you have continued to see each other the whole time Presley and Will have been married."

"Pretty much." This time when he reached for the beer he knocked it off the table. He swore a few times, then kicked the can across the room and turned his attention back to his cigarette.

"Did she say anything recently about wishing she'd never had Polly?"

Melissa stared at Jonathan. Though he didn't turn toward her he felt the heat of her glare on him. But the question was necessary.

"Nah." Johnny Ray put his feet on the coffee table. "She didn't really want to be a mother, but she loves the kid the best she knows how."

"No other vehicles were parked near the house when you picked her up or dropped her off that night? You saw no sign of anything out of the ordinary?" Jonathan doubted the man had paid any attention, but this was the only way to find out. He insisted Presley had exited and then reentered the front door, yet the back door was the one found unlocked and open the next morning.

Several tense moments elapsed with Johnny Ray mulling over the question. "Nope, I can't say that I noticed anything. Most of the neighbors were probably in bed. I looked around for Will's truck but I didn't pay attention to anything else being out of place. I'd probably have noticed, though, since we were sneaking around, you know?"

"Yeah." Jonathan braced for an explosion from Melissa. She wasn't going to like this one. "Has Presley ever mentioned William regretting having a child?"

Surprisingly, Melissa sat stone still. Maybe she was in shock at his audacity.

Johnny Ray shook his head. "Will loves that kid more than he loves anything else—including Presley. She gets a little jealous about that sometimes."

Interesting. "Do you know of anyone else who would want to see William or Presley hurt?" If the missing child wasn't for ransom or trafficking, there had to be another motive. Hurting the family was at the top of the list in Jonathan's opinion.

"Well," Johnny Ray drawled, stretching out in his chair, "since you ask, I'd have to say Scott Rayburn."

"Scott Rayburn is dead," Jonathan reminded him.

"Yeah. Died at that old shack where the kid was being held, the way I heard it."

"That's correct."

"Melissa might not agree with me on this," Bruce continued, "but I always knew that Rayburn had a thing for Will." He gave Jonathan a knowing look. "You know the kind of thing I mean."

Jonathan nodded.

"But this is a small town. Folks don't go in for that, especially his momma and daddy. Rayburn wasn't about to risk his inheritance." He shoved his cigarette butt in the nearest beer can. "Frankly, I'm not surprised he was involved with this somehow. He would've liked nothing better than for Will and Presley to split up. With the kid out of the picture I guess he figured he'd have a better shot at making his lifelong dream come true."

"That is the craziest thing I've ever heard," Melissa said, her voice tight.

Jonathan imagined the real meltdown would come later, when they were out of Bruce's house. She would let him have it then. "Are you speculating," Jonathan pushed, "or do you have proof of this accusation?"

"Let's just say I noticed the way Rayburn looked at William. He idolized the guy." Johnny Ray spat out another of those crude snorts. "Don't for the life of me see why, but I know what I saw. Back in school some of us used to rib Will about his secret admirer."

"Then you believe Rayburn was in on the abduction," Jonathan pressed.

"Maybe, maybe not, but he damned sure knew about it. He couldn't have walked right up on the holding place."

"What about Price?" Jonathan asked. "Do you believe Rayburn was working with Price?"

"It's doubtful," Johnny Ray said with expanding self-importance. The drugs had obviously kicked in full gear. "Scott thought he was above working with what he considered lesser life forms. To him Stevie was pretty much a worm or something."

Melissa didn't defend Price as she had before. Didn't take a psychology degree to analyze her reason. Price had had something to do with Polly's abduction.

"Someone else was involved," Jonathan went on. "The shooter who killed Rayburn and Price. Any guesses on that one?"

"My uncle figures Rayburn shot Price, since the shotgun they found in the river belonged to him."

This was news to Jonathan. He wasn't aware the weapon had been retrieved.

Johnny Ray put his hand over his mouth. "I don't think I was supposed to tell that to anyone."

What else was the chief holding out on them? "The chief keeps me fully briefed," Jonathan lied. "You haven't shared anything I didn't know."

"Well then you know that old Stevie had a piece of Rayburn's shirt clutched in his cold, dead hand. Them two most likely struggled before the gun fired."

More news. "That hasn't been confirmed," Jonathan said so as to sound knowledgeable of the details.

"Maybe not," Johnny Ray said, "but if my uncle said that's the way it went down, then that's the way it went down. He's been doing this a long time. He knows his stuff."

"You can't think of anyone else who might have wanted to hurt the Shepherd family?" Jonathan asked again.

Johnny Ray shook his head. "Not a soul. The whole town seems to look up to the Shepherds. Don't know why." He leered at Melissa. "They aren't that smart or that pretty."

Jonathan pushed to his feet. "I'll come back if I think of any more questions."

Now he was the one ready to go off. Kicking the butt of a man already injured shouldn't feel so appealing but Johnny Ray Bruce evidently could care less whom he angered. He likely assumed his uncle's position would continue to keep him out of trouble with the law. But one of these days his mouth was going to get him killed. His uncle wouldn't be able to get him out of that.

Melissa walked ahead of Jonathan toward the car, her movements stilted. Once they were inside, with the doors closed, she held up both hands. "If I'd had a weapon, I think I would have killed that egotistical SOB."

Backing out of the drive, Jonathan suggested, "That would be letting him off too easily." He didn't mention that he'd had the same passing thought himself.

"He's out of his mind."

"Perhaps. Pain meds do that sometimes."

Melissa glared at him. He got it. She would know. He hadn't needed to make that point.

"You're not buying his tale of unrequited love where Rayburn and Will are concerned?"

"Not really, but we can't rule it out, either."

Melissa made a sound that warned that he'd given the wrong answer.

Jonathan set a course for Rayburn's office. He'd already checked the address and determined the route. Knowing Melissa, he'd expected her to be angry with him, so he'd come prepared.

"Surely you don't believe him over me," Melissa demanded when Jonathan failed to retract his statement.

"In my experience," he said, hoping she wouldn't burn off any more of her pent up anger on him, "where there's smoke, there's fire. Rumors usually are seeded in some semblance of the truth."

She dropped her head back on the seat. "I don't believe it at all. I never saw or heard anything to that effect."

"Do you know Ms. O'Linger?"

"Yes." She sighed. "She was my English teacher in high school. She retired a few years ago and started working with Scott."

"Why don't you handle this one," Jonathan suggested.

"What am I supposed to ask?" Melissa didn't sound enthused by the offer. "I'm certainly not going to ask her if she thought Scott had a crush on Will."

"The answers you need will prompt the questions." That was Jonathan's method. There was no reason to ask a question unless the answer would serve a purpose. "I don't expect you to ask her about that part."

"Good. Because I won't."

Having Melissa ask the questions of a former teacher might garner more answers. If nothing else, the effort would make Melissa feel more useful, lessening the likelihood that she would work up another head of steam. She was already going to be angry enough when they moved on to the third name on his list.

Ms. O'LINGER CRIED twice before Melissa and Jonathan were settled in Scott Rayburn's office. The woman was beside herself with grief. She couldn't imagine why anyone would want to hurt Scotty, as she called him. And he assuredly never had anything to do with Polly's disappearance. More likely he'd stumbled upon the truth and set out to investigate. Ms. O'Linger hadn't been able to bring herself to leave the office—even on Sunday—until she'd set everything to rights after the chief's search.

"Do you have reason to believe Scott was investigating Polly's disappearance?" Melissa asked.

Jonathan flashed a look of approval. He'd been correct when he'd said she would know the questions to ask. That he had faith in her ability to do the job made her feel a little better. Took her mind off poor Uncle Harry lying in that hospital bed.

Ms. O'Linger collapsed into the leather executive chair behind Scott's desk. "Mercy, let me think." She rubbed at her forehead. "I'm just so confused. I can hardly believe this has happened."

Melissa held her breath, hoping the woman could give them something, anything, that might help.

Ms. O'Linger pinched her lips together and glanced at Jonathan.

"Jonathan is here to help," Melissa assured the

woman. "He's my friend." She'd introduced him that way, but evidently the message hadn't gotten through.

"I'm sure he's very nice," Ms. O'Linger agreed, "but the chief made me promise not to talk about this to anyone." She wrung her hands. "He went over Scotty's office and house. His momma and daddy were awfully upset as it was..." She shook her head. "But when the chief questioned me, he specifically said not to discuss what I knew with anyone. Not a soul."

Anticipation fired in Melissa's veins. "Ms. O'Linger, you've known me your whole life. I just want to find my niece. We're not planning to get in the chief's way. We want to help."

The old woman divided her attention between Melissa and Jonathan, her gaze sweeping back and forth repeatedly. "If he finds out I told you..."

"He won't find out," Melissa said quickly. "You have my word on that. You know I took care of Mr. O'Linger in the hospital. You know you can trust me." Ms. O'Linger had been most grateful for Melissa's help during those agonizing final days of her husband's life. That should account for something.

"Yes, you surely did and that's the only reason I'm having second thoughts on following the chief's orders." She shrugged her rounded shoulders. "Truth is, I don't think it's really about the case. The reason he doesn't want me to talk about it, I mean. I think it's just embarrassing to him."

Melissa sat up straighter. The allegations Scott had thrown at Jonathan sifted to the top of her worried mind. Could there be any truth to that rumor? Impossible! Harry would never—Melissa stopped herself. He'd proven her wrong already. At this point, she couldn't say what he or anyone else might be capable of doing.

Even herself. She'd made love with Jonathan when she'd sworn she would never make that mistake again.

"I didn't say anything to Scotty," his secretary admitted with a sheepish look. "I knew he wouldn't like me going through his briefcase. But he left it on his desk and papers were poking out. I only wanted to straighten up for him." She smiled at Melissa. "To me, you're all still just a bunch of kids who need a little extra mothering from time to time."

The urge to prompt her to get on with her story nearly drove Melissa to jump up and shake her. She didn't know how Jonathan stayed so calm when he questioned people.

"Anyway, I found a notepad where he'd scribbled several times and dates." She frowned. "I was curious because I wasn't aware that he'd taken any new cases that involved a divorce with a cheating spouse." She smiled proudly. "He liked following up on those personally."

Melissa sat on the edge of her seat, used her posture to urge the old woman to get on with it.

"But this was no divorce case," Ms. O'Linger

said. "He'd been following Carol Talbot and Harry Shepherd around." She ducked her head toward one shoulder. "Of course I didn't question him about it, but it did appear obvious from his notes that he believed the two were carrying on an—" she looked around the room "—affair."

"Did you give that notepad to the chief?" Jonathan interjected.

Ms. O'Linger nodded. "Oh, yes. He insisted on having it. Scotty had locked it in his safe." She pointed to the floor. "He had that installed right after I came to work for him. He gave me the combination with strict instructions that I was never to open it unless it was an emergency."

"Was there anything else inside?" Melissa asked, her head spinning at the idea that her uncle might actually have been having an affair with his best friend's wife.

How could she have known these people her whole life and not suspected a thing?

"Nothing else," Ms. O'Linger assured her. "Just that notepad."

"Did you look at it before you gave it to the chief?" Jonathan prodded.

Ms. O'Linger's cheeks pinked. "Well, I didn't really mean to, but I guess curiosity got the better of me."

"Had he made any recent entries?" Melissa pressed.

"Yes." The older woman swiped at the desk. "He was going to that old shack again."

"The one next to the river?" Jonathan asked for clarification.

She nodded. "Yes."

"Did he note why he wanted to go there?" Melissa asked, her heart pounding so hard she could scarcely hear herself think.

Sad eyes settled on Melissa. "He was going back to see what was there. He'd followed your uncle to the shack earlier that evening."

The remainder of the conversation was lost on Melissa. Jonathan continued to chat with Ms. O'Linger, but Melissa zoned out completely.

Her uncle had gone to the shack *before* Scott Rayburn's murder.

*Before* Stevie's murder.

He'd gone to that rickety old shack. The one where the police had found evidence indicating that Polly had been held there for at least several days.

Harry Shepherd—the man who had been like a father to her—had taken Polly.

## Chapter Fourteen

"This won't do any good."

Melissa ignored Jonathan's remark. She didn't care. She needed to do this.

As soon as the car was in Park, she wrenched open the door and hurried across the parking lot. This hospital was her home several days a week. No one was going to prevent her from getting in to see her uncle. Now. This minute. She had to talk to him. Whether he could answer her or not didn't matter.

In the lobby she didn't wait for the elevator. She took the stairs. Jonathan climbed right behind her.

"Melissa," he called out, "don't go in there like this."

He didn't understand. Polly wasn't his niece. Jonathan Foley had never connected on that level with anyone. He couldn't know.

As soon as the thought formed in her brain she felt guilty.

But that wasn't stopping her from doing this.

Nothing was.

"Melissa, wait!" head nurse Patty Wheeler cried as Melissa charged past the station on the ICU floor.

She ignored her, as well.

"Wait!" the nurse called again.

"Melissa, stop." Jonathan caught her by the arm.

She shook off his hold. "No. I have to do this."

Before the nurse could catch up to her, Melissa barged into the ICU cubicle—and stalled.

Her uncle's bed was empty. The sheets had been rolled into a ball.

Denial rammed into her with the same impact as butting a brick wall at a full run.

"Melissa, I'm sorry." The nurse, breathless from the rush, put her arm around her. "We tried to call your cell. Your uncle passed away twenty minutes ago."

The world tilted and bitter bile rushed up into Melissa's throat.

"I've got her."

Jonathan's arms were suddenly around her. Patty was asking Melissa questions but she couldn't answer.

Her uncle was gone.

As much as that hurt, what hurt even more was the idea that he may have taken Polly's whereabouts with him.

How would they ever find her now?

*12:15 p.m.*

JONATHAN HAD DONE SOME research while Melissa gathered her composure, curled up in an easy chair in her living room. If Harry Shepherd had been having an affair with Carol Talbot, what were the chances that she had suspected he was up to something?

If they were close, really close, had he shared his plans with her?

In Jonathan's estimation, the most likely motive was diverting William's orders. From all accounts, Harry had been beside himself when William joined the military. He'd basically come unglued when the orders for deployment had come down. Having his nephew survive six months was more than he'd hoped for, but having him go back was unthinkable.

How far would a man go to keep a loved one out of harm's way? Jonathan had never loved anyone like that. He glanced at Melissa, who was attempting to force down a glass of iced tea.

He couldn't love anyone like that. It wasn't in him.

He wanted to. He stole another glance at her. He surely wanted to. But she would be the one to pay for that indulgence. If he'd ever possessed the ability to love that deeply, he'd lost it during those endless hours as he'd watched his men die one by one.

*Focus, Jonathan. This isn't about you.*

The chief had called and royally chewed out Jonathan for what he called interfering with his investigation. His anger had nothing to do with the investigation. Chief Talbot was furious that Jonathan and Melissa had learned the truth about his wife's affair. He had warned them both to stay out of the investigation. Apparently he'd already warned most of Bay Minette's citizens not to talk to Jonathan or Melissa.

William wasn't even speaking to Melissa. He'd gone to the funeral home to make arrangements for his uncle and had outright refused to allow Melissa to accompany him.

Whatever the chief had told William, it had worked. For now.

Jonathan had no intention of allowing this case to go unsolved any more than he intended to allow Melissa to be treated like the bad guy. She had a right to know the truth. And if William weren't so riddled with grief over his daughter's disappearance and his uncle's suicide, he would see that.

"What do we do now?"

Jonathan met her gaze. Those big blue eyes held more pain than any one human should have to bear. "We move on to the one logical remaining person of interest."

Melissa nodded. "Carol Talbot."

"The chief's actions aren't completely consistent with those of a man who wants to protect his wife's reputation. He's certainly protecting her in every other way. But not on this count. He could easily refute the allegations by charging that Harry had been delusional and suggested these things to Rayburn as a result of those delusions. Harry isn't here to defend himself or to say otherwise. Neither is Rayburn."

"You think there's more."

Jonathan didn't want to give Melissa false hope, but she needed the truth right now. He couldn't ensure she got that from anyone else, but she was getting it from him. "My guess is he doesn't want her to become more collateral damage in this case. Four people are dead. Polly is still missing. And no one knows a damned thing, particularly the police who are investigating the case."

"That makes sense." Melissa shrugged. "Both he and Carol could deny the affair." She closed her eyes and exhaled a heavy breath. "I didn't have a clue. I doubt very many others did, either. Now the chief just wants to protect her from what? Accessory to murder? Conspiracy to commit kidnapping?"

"Exactly. Otherwise, why go to such lengths?" The more they discussed the theory, the more convinced Jonathan grew that the chief was covering for something his wife either knew or had done.

"There's no logical reason." The same realization that had dawned on him widened Melissa's eyes. "She knows something. Saw something." Melissa turned her hands up. "Something that could make her appear guilty."

"That's my thinking."

Fear abruptly froze in her eyes. "Oh, God. She may know…" Melissa hugged her arms around her middle. "She may have witnessed someone hurting Polly. May have had some part in it." Melissa looked ready to crumple emotionally. "He's definitely protecting her from any criminal charges."

Jonathan went to her. He knelt in front of her and took her shoulders in his hands, gave her a gentle shake. "We don't know that. All we can be relatively certain of is that she knows something. We're going to operate on the theory that Polly is alive and out there somewhere waiting to be found. Carol may be able to lead us to her."

Melissa searched his eyes. He tried to show her the hope, the certainty he felt, but she shook her head. "If that's all she knows—Polly's location—why wouldn't the chief just go get Polly and tell the world that his amazing investigative skills are responsible for solving the case? No one would ever know his wife told him where to look. It's worse than that. I can feel it."

Jonathan couldn't deny that possibility. "For now," he urged, "let's not lose hope."

Melissa laughed but the sound was filled with pain. "This coming from the man who wouldn't give me the slightest inkling of hope that he could ever love me?" She shook her head. "Jonathan, I don't know how I'd have gotten through this so far without your help." She touched his face, just the slightest caress of his jaw. "But I know you too well. You can't love me the way I love you. You said so yourself. I appreciate that you're trying to keep me bolstered now in this awful, awful time. But don't pretend you know what you're talking about when it comes to hope."

She shook her head. "Or that kind of love. The kind that would make a man go against the grain of all he is to protect the woman he loves the way Chief Talbot is obviously doing for his wife."

Jonathan stood. "I can't deny those charges." He crossed the room and stared out the window. He'd never been any good at moments like this, but he had to try.

Whatever his and Melissa's past, whatever their present, a child was missing and by God he intended to do whatever he could to find her.

"Let's go." He pushed aside the unfamiliar emotions she'd stirred and put on his game face. There was a job to do and he wasn't about to fall down on getting it done. That he could guarantee.

She pushed to her feet and reached for her purse. "The chief will try to stop us."

"It won't be the first time someone tried to stop me."

Jonathan opened the door for her. His chest squeezed at the scent of her as she walked past him on her way out the door. He booted the sensation aside and followed her. When this was done, he would go back to Chicago and she could get on with her life.

He hoped she found a man who could feel those emotions she cherished so.

That man wasn't him. He'd known that before he'd answered her plea for help.

She had known it, as well.

CHIEF TALBOT'S HOUSE sat on a side street just off the main thoroughfare. Neat houses lined the street, but only one had a large moving truck parked out front.

Melissa was out of the car before Jonathan could shut down the engine. Every word she'd said to him was true. But in the silence on the drive over here those words had gotten to him anyway. Left him feeling empty and aching.

Strange for a guy who prided himself on feeling nothing.

He caught up with Melissa on the sidewalk. She marched right up to the house and walked through the open door.

"Where's Mrs. Talbot?" she demanded of one of the men who were obviously movers.

The man shrugged. "The owners aren't here."

Melissa turned to Jonathan. "We just spoke to the chief a few hours ago. They can't have suddenly disappeared."

Jonathan hitched a thumb toward the street. "Where are the Talbots moving to?"

Another of the movers stopped his work and scratched his head. "Gatlinburg. Up in northeast Tennessee. We're supposed to have all this—" he gestured to the boxes and furnishings "—up there by tomorrow."

Jonathan and Melissa exchanged a glance. "Has Mrs. Talbot already left for the new house?" she asked.

"Don't know." He nodded toward the door. "You can ask him. He's the owner."

Jonathan turned to face the chief. The shade of red coloring his face warned that he was not happy to find the two of them there.

"You're trespassing on private property, Mr. Foley."

His voice was far too quiet, far too controlled. "We came to see Mrs. Talbot." No point in lying. "We have a few questions about Harry Shepherd for her."

The chief ignored Jonathan's statement and shifted his attention to Melissa. "Now, Melissa, I know you're all torn up and that's completely understandable. But you've got to talk some sense into your friend. When I give an order I expect folks to follow it. I'm doing all I can to find little Polly. But I can't do that if I have to keep an eye on the two of you."

Melissa shook her head. "Sorry, Chief." Tears spilled down her cheeks. "I just can't believe Uncle Harry killed himself and I thought maybe Mrs. Talbot could help me understand what was going through his mind. It's just so awful."

Jonathan had to hand it to her, she'd even fooled him there for a second.

Chief Talbot patted her on the shoulder. "I'll see what I can find out. I'm hoping something Harry confided in her will give us some clue as to where Polly is. Carol has been a good friend to him through all this." He shook his head. "I still can't understand what he was doing. Maybe Price and Rayburn were up to no good and Harry found out. They may have taken little Polly to blackmail Harry. We just don't know yet. But you have my word that I won't stop until I know the whole truth."

He puffed out a weary breath. "Right now, I need your help. This has been real hard on Carol, too. She never has gotten over our little Sherry's death. Polly's disappearance and all that mess over at the river have torn her all to pieces. That's why she moved on up to the new house. She needed to get away from this tragedy to save her peace of mind." He patted Melissa again. "But don't worry, I'm not going anywhere until we find Polly and this case is sewed up. You have my word on that."

"Thank you, Chief." Melissa swiped her eyes. "I know you'll be glad to retire like you'd planned and join your wife."

"Yes, ma'am, but not until my job here is done."

*11:18 p.m.*

"YOU'RE SURE THAT'S IT?" Melissa peered up at the grand log house. "I can't believe the chief was able to buy something like this up here." Housing prices in the Gatlinburg area were far higher than those down in Bay Minette.

"It's the one." Jonathan shoved his cell phone into his pocket. "According to my sources—"

His sources. He never gave up names. She'd overheard far too many of his conversations back when they were together.

"—the chief has saved a serious chunk of change during his career. He also recently sold the property near the river."

Melissa cringed at the thought of that river. Polly hadn't been found in the water but she could still be out there somewhere.

"I don't remember hearing about that." But then she wasn't one to listen to gossip or rumors. She focused on work, taking all the overtime the hospital would allow. She'd saved quite a chunk of change, as he put it, herself over the past three years. As much as she loved the Shepherd home, she'd always hoped to move on with her life. Maybe go back to Birmingham or Montgomery. Maybe even Huntsville. But with Will, Polly and Harry, the concept just kept fading into the future.

Harry was gone now. Her heart squeezed at the thought. Whatever he'd done the final days of his life, he'd been a good uncle to her and Will for most of their lives.

All the emotions associated with his death would have to be sorted out later…when Polly was home.

Or buried.

She closed her eyes and exiled the thought. Polly had to be alive. All they needed was someone to tell them where Harry had taken her…and why. That last part wasn't entirely necessary, but it would be nice to know why he'd done this. She could guess, as Jonathan had, but she needed to know.

Jonathan hadn't said much on the way here. She couldn't blame him. She'd said some awful things to him. Most had been true, but she'd been raised better than to say something hurtful.

"Someone's home," Jonathan said, pointing to the massive front windows on the first floor.

Melissa squinted to make out the figure moving around in what she presumed to be the main living area. "That's Carol."

Carol moved about the room, but Melissa couldn't determine what she was doing. Putting things away maybe? Didn't seem likely since the moving truck hadn't arrived. The movers had said they were expected tomorrow.

Carol stopped suddenly, picked something up from what appeared to be a table and placed it against her ear.

Melissa stared harder. A phone. Cell phone probably, judging by its size.

Carol started to move around again.

"She's pacing."

"Looks that way," Melissa agreed.

Carol abruptly stopped once more, directly in front of the big windows. She seemed to stare out into the dark night. Melissa resisted the impulse to hunker down in the seat. She couldn't possibly see them. The tree-crowded drive Jonathan had selected was well hidden. They'd driven all the way up to the house across the road from the Talbot place and no one had been home. Several newspapers had lain on the porch suggesting the owners were on vacation. Parking at the end of the drive gave Melissa and Jonathan a perfect view of the new Talbot home.

Carol reached up and tugged on something.

"What's she doing?" Melissa murmured.

Heavy drapes glided across the windows, blocking their view into the house.

"That call must've been from the chief." Jonathan checked the road in both directions. "He's probably on his way here."

They had known that as soon as Chief Talbot figured out they had left town he would likely follow or he would send one of his deputies to stop them. Apparently he hadn't learned of their departure quickly enough to stop them en route.

"We should go to the door and talk to her before the chief or whomever he sends gets here." Melissa was terrified they'd come all this way for nothing. If the chief got here he would ensure they didn't get close to the house.

Jonathan turned to her in the darkness. She couldn't see his face but she could feel the tension emanating from him. "You realize that once we set foot on their property, we're breaking the law. The chief isn't likely to let us off with a warning this time."

"I don't care." The law wasn't going to stop her

from talking to Carol Talbot. Not unless they locked Melissa away where she couldn't get out.

"Let's do it then."

Jonathan reached under the seat and removed something that he stuffed under his shirt.

"What's that?" She was almost afraid of the answer.

"We can't go in without protection." Before she could argue, he added, "I have a license to carry this weapon. I'm an expert marksman. I'm not going to shoot anyone unless they try to shoot one of us first."

Melissa took a tight breath as she squeezed the door handle. "You think we should just call the FBI or something?" Second thoughts burrowed deep into her brain.

"And tell them what?"

"That we believe Carol Talbot knows something about Polly's disappearance." It might be worth a try.

"And when she says she doesn't, what then?"

Jonathan was right. "Okay, let's go." Melissa opened the door. The interior light didn't come on since Jonathan had adjusted it to stay off.

If they hurried, maybe they could talk to Carol before anyone else arrived.

Jonathan led the way through the darkness, across the road and up the hill upon which the Talbot house proudly sat. It was cooler in the mountains. Melissa wished she had brought a jacket.

"We're going around to the back," Jonathan whispered to her. "There isn't a security system yet, so we don't have to worry about that."

Confusion muddled Melissa's focus again. "How do you know this?"

"I have sources."

"Right." How could she have forgotten?

Jonathan stayed within the shadows of the trees that bordered the big yard. Once they reached the rear of the house, he grabbed her hand and darted toward a clump of designer shrubbery that provided some amount of protection from the landscape lighting.

They stayed put for a few seconds, long enough to assume they hadn't been spotted, then he hauled her all the way to the corner of the house.

Melissa struggled to keep her respiration slow and deep. Her heart was beating so fast she could hardly draw in a deep breath. Jonathan's firm grip on her hand was all that kept her courage in place.

As long as she was with him, she could do this.

Lights were on all over the house. Was Carol Talbot afraid of being here alone?

Jonathan pulled Melissa forward, staying close against the back of the house. At the first window they reached, he listened for a moment, then peeked inside.

When he'd flattened against the house again, she asked, "Anything?"

He shook his head. "Empty room."

They moved forward again, checked a couple more

windows. Nothing. When they rounded the corner at the other end of the house, the window was too high for Jonathan to see inside. If they could determine exactly where Carol was, she couldn't pretend not to be there when they pounded on the door. They needed her to know that they knew she was in the house.

"I'll get on your shoulders," Melissa whispered.

He considered her suggestion a moment, then dropped to his knees. Melissa climbed into a sitting position on his shoulders and he slowly pushed to his feet. She leaned a little to her left to avoid being in full view of the window.

Once he had braced against the house, she leaned a little the other way and peeked inside.

There was a bed in this room, and a suitcase. Melissa stretched her neck to see more of the room without exposing any more of her body than necessary. But she saw nothing else.

The door to the room opened, and Melissa's breath stalled in her lungs.

She knew she should move, should somehow signal Jonathan to lower her down, but she couldn't react. She remained frozen, watching as Carol Talbot entered the room.

The elegant looking woman walked toward the mattress and patted it as she said something Melissa couldn't quite make out.

Carol repeated the actions, and a child walked hesitantly through the door.

Melissa's heart skipped a beat.

*Polly.*

Carol Talbot whipped around to stare at the window. That was when Melissa knew she'd said the name aloud.

Carol snatched up Polly and ran from the room.

"She's here!" Melissa shouted. She tried to get down. Her sudden movement toppled both her and Jonathan to the ground.

Melissa scrambled up. "Polly's here!" she cried as she ran around to the front corner of the house.

"Melissa, wait!" Jonathan called after her.

Melissa didn't stop. She couldn't wait. Polly was inside. She was alive.

She hit the front steps in a dead run. Jonathan passed her on the way up and banged on the door. "Carol Talbot, we know you're in there! Open the door!"

Melissa shoved her fingers into the front pocket of her jeans and fumbled to pull out her cell phone.

Jonathan rammed his shoulder into the door. The entire frame shook. "Open the door, Mrs. Talbot!"

Melissa started entering the numbers. 9…1…

Jonathan hit the door again and it burst inward.

Melissa forgot about calling for help. She rushed past Jonathan and headed for the room at the north end of the house.

Jonathan caught up with her, passed her, shoving her behind him as he went.

"Stop right there or I'll shoot."

Carol Talbot huddled in the hallway, Polly wrapped in her arms, her face pressed to Carol's chest. The gun in Carol's hand shook, but its intended aim was unmistakable.

Melissa ceased to breathe.

Jonathan held out his hands in a placating manner. "Put the gun down, Mrs. Talbot."

She shook her head. "No. You're not going to take her."

Polly whimpered. Melissa's chest constricted.

"Mrs. Talbot," Jonathan reasoned, "her parents are waiting for her back home. You need to let her go now and we'll work this out. I'm certain you intended her no harm."

Carol shook her head adamantly once more. "Leave or I will shoot."

Melissa stepped forward. "Then you're going to have to shoot me, because I'm taking my niece home."

Jonathan reached for Melissa, but she stepped beyond his reach.

"Stop!" Carol shouted.

"I'm sorry, Mrs. Talbot," Melissa said, "but you can't keep Polly. I appreciate that you've taken such good care of her. But you have to let her go home now."

Polly cried out, apparently recognizing her aunt Melissa's voice. She wiggled in an attempt to get free. Carol held her tighter, kept the weapon aimed at Melissa.

"Shhh, Polly, it'll be okay now," Melissa murmured.

"Leave my home," Carol demanded. "Before I'm forced to do something I don't want to do."

"Mrs. Talbot," Jonathan urged, "think about what you're doing. This whole thing was Harry's idea. You aren't the one who took Polly. You tried to help. That's what we'll tell the police."

Carol blinked. "That's what I told my husband." She tightened her grip on the weapon. "Harry almost lost his mind when William went off to Afghanistan. But when William came home it only got worse. Harry kept saying he had to do something. He took Polly that night. Had Stevie watching her. Everything would have worked out perfectly if that fool Scott Rayburn hadn't gotten in the way. I had to kill him. He was going to ruin everything."

Melissa nodded, following Jonathan's cue. "You had no choice. You tried to protect Polly and Harry."

Carol made a keening sound. "It would have been so perfect. William would have seen Presley for what she was and gotten rid of her, then if he was forced to deploy, Harry and I would have taken care of Polly." Her hold on Polly tightened. The little girl fretted.

"You loved Harry," Melissa said softly. "And he loved you." The kind of love these two had shared had twisted their minds, pushed them over some sort of ledge.

"He was too weak to handle what needed to be

done." Carol lifted her chin in defiance. "Now I have to do it. Presley isn't fit to be the mother of this child and William is hardly any better. Sherry needs a real family. One who will love and take care of her."

*Sherry.* She thought Polly was her daughter.

"Mrs. Talbot," Melissa said, "this is Polly, not Sherry."

Carol blinked as if she didn't understand. In that moment of distraction, Polly darted out of her hold. Carol screamed at her to come back, but the girl ran down the hall to Melissa.

Melissa knelt down and wrapped her arms around the child.

"You won't take her!" Carol shouted. Grasping the weapon with both hands, she aimed it at Melissa and Polly.

Jonathan slammed into Melissa, knocking her and Polly to the floor, just as a bullet exploded from the weapon, echoing through the house.

Crouched over Polly, Melissa heard the sounds of struggling. Jonathan was attempting to subdue Carol. She held Polly close to her chest and scooted away from the danger.

As another shot rang out, Melissa reached into her pocket for her cell phone. Not there. Had she dropped it?

Carol screamed, and the weapon fired again.

She chanced a glance over her shoulder and saw Jonathan fling himself atop the woman.

Melissa jumped to her feet. She had to do something.

She rushed into the closest room, put Polly in the closet. "Stay right here, Polly. Don't move." She closed the door, winced at the child's sobbing.

Frantic, Melissa looked around. There was nothing to use as a weapon... Her gaze lit on the heavy curtain rod above the window.

She snatched it down and rushed into the corridor.

Jonathan had Carol pinned to the floor. "Call for help," he yelled out to Melissa.

She dropped the curtain rod and ran back to the front door to search for her phone. She found it on the steps. She grabbed it and completed the call she had started minutes before.

Once she'd given the dispatcher their location, she rushed back to where Jonathan continued to restrain Carol.

"I'll try to find something to tie her up," Melissa offered.

Jonathan nodded.

That was when she saw the blood.

It soaked his shirt in a long line starting at his shoulder.

Her heart bumped her sternum.

*Pull it together.*

She ran to the bedroom where she'd seen the suitcase. The zipper gave her hell, but she finally ripped the bag open. Melissa grabbed several items and hurried back to the hall.

Trying not to rough Carol up too much, they got her restrained, with the clothing as makeshift rope.

Melissa hurried back to the closet where she'd left Polly. She lifted the little girl into her arms and hugged her tight. "It's okay now."

Polly sobbed against her chest. Melissa kissed her sweet head, inhaled the baby scent of her silky blond hair. "Thank God. Thank God." It would be okay now.

Except for Jonathan. How badly was he hurt? Polly in tow, she hurried back to the hall. "We should look at—"

Chief Talbot stood in the hallway, his weapon leveled on Jonathan.

Fear grabbed Melissa by the throat.

Jonathan was attempting to talk him into putting the weapon down. Melissa was too terrified to move. If he turned the gun on her he might hit Polly.

"Your wife is going to need your help, Chief," Jonathan offered. "You need to be able to help her. You can't do that if you don't make the right choice now."

Carol lay on the floor bellowing in agony, her hands and feet tied behind her.

Chief Talbot turned to Melissa. Her breath caught.

"I'm sorry." He shook his head. "I thought I could make this right."

With the gun trained on Jonathan, time seemed to stand still.

Then finally Chief Talbot lowered his weapon, bent down and placed it on the floor.

Melissa dragged in a breath.

It was over.

Jonathan took the chief's weapon and ushered him over to take care of his wife. Then he came to Melissa and his arms went around her.

It was really over.

Polly was safe.

The smell of warm blood filtered into her nostrils. Melissa drew back. "You're hurt. Let me look at that."

He didn't resist. They walked outside, away from the chief and his wife and their sobbing. Those two had their own problems to work out.

Melissa settled Jonathan on the front steps with Polly right next to him and inspected the bullet wound.

"It's not so bad," she surmised. "Right in and right out. Based on the location in your shoulder, it shouldn't have hit anything important."

Jonathan looked up at her. "Easy for you to say. You're not the one bleeding."

Melissa smiled. "You'll live, trust me."

He took her hand in his. "I do trust you."

The pain in his eyes was not from the wound; that she knew for sure. "I'm glad you still can after all I said."

"It was all true."

God, she'd said some awful things to him. "I'm sorry. I was...overwrought."

"You told the truth." He squeezed her hand. "But there's always room for change. Even for a guy like me."

She nodded, the movement like the workings of a rusty hinge. Words would not squeeze past the emotion in her throat. It was all she could do to hold back the tears.

"Give me another chance," he murmured.

For three years she had hoped one day he would say those words. "I'm sorry." She sucked in a jagged breath. "Could you repeat that, please?"

He laughed. But before he could, Polly tugged at Melissa's blouse. "I want my daddy."

Melissa laughed and cried at the same time. She scooped the child into her arms. "I will definitely take you to your mommy and daddy, little one."

Jonathan pulled her down to sit beside him. He kissed her cheek and rubbed Polly's pretty head.

They were okay. Melissa felt herself smiling again. They were better than okay.

Blue lights flashed in the distance.

"Those guys should have a first aid kit." She was still worried about Jonathan's injury despite her assessment.

"I'll be fine."

Good grief, she was a nurse. She should be taking care of him not the other way around. But right now her head was spinning wildly. Her heart was thumping like crazy and she couldn't think.

He lifted her chin, ushering her gaze to his. "Think about my offer, would you?"

She bit her lips together for a moment to hold back the tears. "There's nothing to think about. You're on, Mr. Foley." She narrowed her gaze. "But I'm warning you, you won't get away so easily this time."

He smiled. It reached all the way to her heart. "Don't worry. I'm not going anywhere without you."

## Chapter Fifteen

*Chicago, Monday, May 30th, 1:30 p.m.*

"So this is the real Jonathan Foley?" Melissa bit her lips together to hide a smile as she surveyed the place Jonathan called home.

He quirked an eyebrow at her. He loved it when her eyes sparkled so. "I'm rarely here." But that sad fact was about to change.

Melissa strolled over to the table next to the sofa and pointed to the blinking light on his answering machine. He had fourteen messages. "Are those girlfriends?" She smiled this time but there was a little hesitancy in her eyes. She still needed some reassurance.

Jonathan crossed to where she stood and pulled her into his arms. "My boss or one of my colleagues." He brushed his lips over hers. She gasped. "Probably trying to persuade me not to go."

She searched his eyes, hers full of hope. "You're sure this is what you want to do?"

"Absolutely." He kissed her nose, his body already

reacting to holding her near. "My boss hired a new staff when he bought the Equalizer shop. None of the former staff stayed. He's got a couple of really top-notch guys who can handle things until he replaces me. He won't even miss me."

Her gorgeous face brightened with happiness and his heart stumbled. Finally, he'd been able to do what he couldn't three years ago—make her happy. That meant more to him than he could possibly ever hope to articulate.

"Well, let's get you packed!"

She started to pull out of his arms, but he drew her closer. They'd come straight here from the airport. He had to pack up and turn in his keys to the landlord. "Later." He grinned. "We haven't slowed down since we found Polly. I'd like a few minutes with you all to myself."

"Sounds doable." She tiptoed and nipped his bottom lip with her teeth. "We're known for slow and easy in the south."

"Then I'm going to love living in Alabama." He covered her mouth with his own. She melted into him.

The telephone rang.

Jonathan reluctantly drew back enough to take a breath. "Do we really need a phone in Alabama?"

Melissa laughed. "We'll have to negotiate that."

The answering machine picked up and the voice of his former boss from the Equalizers filled the silence.

"Your final case has been closed out, Foley. Good luck in your new endeavor." The line disconnected.

"Now—" Jonathan cupped her face "—where were we?"

*3:30 p.m.*

SLADE CLOSED THE FILE he'd been reviewing. The assignment was exactly the sort of case Dakota Garrett could handle. Ex Special Forces. Kicked out of the military for disobeying orders. Definitely the right man for the job. No worries there.

He closed the file and turned off the light on his desk. He locked up on his way out of the brownstone. He never visited the office unless his secretary was gone for the day or away on lunch. Never met face-to-face with his investigators. For now that was the way it had to stay.

Since Foley had resigned, Slade would need to consider a new hire. None of the former owner's staff had remained with the Equalizers firm. Not that Slade wanted anyone who knew the former owner, Jim Colby, to stay. Still, he needed to keep the Equalizers operational until he was finished here. Staying operational required staff.

Slade pointed his SUV in the direction of downtown. He had something to do. The same thing he did every day at this time. His destination had a transit time of about twenty minutes, depending upon traffic. Once at the location, he parked his SUV and then parked himself at the same table he always chose at Maggie's Coffee House.

The table provided the best view of the comings and goings at the Colby Agency. He placed his same order, medium black coffee, dark Columbian roast. Then he settled in to observe his prey.

No one at the Colby Agency knew him. Even Jim, the man from whom he'd bought the brownstone and the Equalizers firm, didn't know his name or his face.

Slade Keaton wasn't even his real name.

He hadn't used that sham of a name in over a decade. He never would again.

Slade had taken charge of his life. He'd clawed his way up from rock bottom and now he owned whatever he chose to own, whomever he chose to own.

And not a soul had a clue who he was or what he was up to. Certainly not anyone at the Colby Agency.

But they would know very soon.

Very, very soon they would all know him.

One of them in particular, the illustrious Lucas Camp, would come face-to-face with that long ago mistake he'd made and quickly forgotten.

And he would pay.

Victoria Colby-Camp had better brace herself.

Her whole perfect world was about to be turned upside down.

\* \* \* \* \*

# ♦ Harlequin®
# INTRIGUE®

## COMING NEXT MONTH

### Available May 10, 2011

**#1275 BABY BOOTCAMP**
*Daddy Corps*
**Mallory Kane**

**#1276 BRANDED**
*Whitehorse, Montana: Chisholm Cattle Company*
**B.J. Daniels**

**#1277 DAMAGED**
*Colby Agency: The New Equalizers*
**Debra Webb**

**#1278 THE MAN FROM GOSSAMER RIDGE**
*Cooper Justice: Cold Case Investigation*
**Paula Graves**

**#1279 UNFORGETTABLE**
**Cassie Miles**

**#1280 BEAR CLAW CONSPIRACY**
*Bear Claw Creek Crime Lab*
**Jessica Andersen**

You can find more information on upcoming
Harlequin® titles, free excerpts and more at
**www.HarlequinInsideRomance.com.**

HICNM0411

*With an evil force hell-bent on destruction,
two enemies must unite to find a truth that turns
all-too-personal when passions collide.*

*Enjoy a sneak peek in Jenna Kernan's next installment
in her original* TRACKER *series, GHOST STALKER,
available in May, only from Harlequin Nocturne.*

"**W**ho are you?" he snarled.

Jessie lifted her chin. "Your better."

His smile was cold. "Such arrogance could only come from a Niyanoka."

She nodded. "Why are you here?"

"I don't know." He glanced about her room. "I asked the birds to take me to a healer."

"And they have done so. Is that *all* you asked?"

"No. To lead them away from my friends." His eyes fluttered and she saw them roll over white.

Jessie straightened, preparing to flee, but he roused himself and mastered the momentary weakness. His eyes snapped open, locking on her.

Her heart hammered as she inched back.

"Lead who away?" she whispered, suddenly afraid of the answer.

"The ghosts. Nagi sent them to attack me so I would bring them to her."

The wolf must be deranged because Nagi did not send ghosts to attack living creatures. He captured the evil ones after their death if they refused to walk the Way of Souls, forcing them to face judgment.

"Her? The healer you seek is also female?"

"Michaela. She's Niyanoka, like you. The last Seer of Souls and Nagi wants her dead."

Jessie fell back to her seat on the carpet as the possibility of this ricocheted in her brain. Could it be true?

"Why should I believe you?" But she knew why. His black aura, the part that said he had been touched by death. Only a ghost could do that. But it made no sense.

Why would Nagi hunt one of her people and why would a Skinwalker want to protect her? She had been trained from birth to hate the Skinwalkers, to consider them a threat.

His intent blue eyes pinned her. Jessie felt her mouth go dry as she considered the impossible. Could the trickster be speaking the truth? Great Mystery, what evil was this?

She stared in astonishment. There was only one way to find her answers. But she had never even met a Skinwalker before and so did not even know if they dreamed.

But if he dreamed, she would have her chance to learn the truth.

*Look for GHOST STALKER by Jenna Kernan,*
*available May only from Harlequin Nocturne,*
*wherever books and ebooks are sold.*

HNEXP0511